Dedicated to every

Thank you!

Other books by this author:

Brackett Hollister: The Werewolf Pack

Copyright ©2014 Quentin Wallace

No part of this work may be reproduced in any form without written permission from the author other than short excerpts used for reviews.

This book is a work of fiction. Names, places, characters, and incidents are fictitious or used fictitiously. Any resemblance to actual persons, living or dead, events or places is entire coincidental.

All Rights Reserved.

First Edition: September 2014

THE GAME WARDEN OF BLACK SWAMP

BY

QUENTIN WALLACE

ONE

The American Revolution, Black Swamp, Georgia, USA

"We're lost," Daniel Barrington said as he rubbed his shoulder through the thick red coat he wore. His regiment had become separated during a skirmish with some American Soldiers and now he, along with his commanding officer and about twenty others, was lost in a swamp near the colony of Georgia. Most of the battles had been fought further north, but in order to quell the rebellion it was determined war would need to be waged all along the eastern seaboard. Therefore, they found themselves in Georgia. Since he had been here, Dan had found Georgia to be nothing but hot, humid and full of biting bugs. Mosquitoes, gnats, and many other unknown insects had raised welts and caused itching on every part of his body. As far as Dan was concerned, Georgia could have its independence and the devil could take this godforsaken land. But he was an army man, and he did as he was told.

"We are not lost, we are simply separated. In time, I am sure we will be reunited with our brethren," Commander Alfred Brown stated with all the arrogance his position afforded him. Most of the men couldn't stand Brown—who had gotten the position only through family connections and not through any acts of his own—but once again, they were loyal to Britain and did as they were told.

"Well, we also appear to be separated from all civilization," Dan said, his irritation showing.

"Come now, we are all soldiers of the King, and therefore this is but a minor setback to us. Let us be on our way,"

Commander Brown said, leading the men off in a direction they were certain he had chosen at random.

As the men stumbled through the swampy mire, they found it getting hotter and more humid with each step, and the ground was also getting softer. After trudging along for what felt like miles, they were finally greeted by an eerie lake by an eerie lake of black water, layered with green vegetation. The mosquitoes were unbearable here and the men found themselves being bitten even through the thick red coats they were wearing. They looked around but could see no way around the water. There were cypress trees, as well as pine trees and great oaks all along the edge of the waterline. The trees served as a canopy for the area, blocking out the sun and creating an eerie shadowed effect. It would seem that the shade should cool the area from the hot sun, but instead it worked as an oven, making this area even hotter as though it held the heat within.

"Now what?" asked Dan, seemingly the only man in the group willing to converse with the Commander.

"Now we travel on through the water. We have to be nearing the ocean, and this water should lead us right to the Atlantic. Once we reach the coastline, we will be able to make our way back to the main force," Commander Brown stated expertly, though he was no expert and really had no idea what he was talking about.

"How do you expect us to make our way through? We have no boats," Dan asked, wondering if he expected them to begin chopping down trees and building rafts.

"We will trudge our way through. These swamps of the south land are never very deep. We can probably walk through easily. We'll need to be careful of the muck on the bottom, and of course watch out for snakes and other fauna, but I'm sure hearty men such as ourselves can make it no problem," Brown said as if his every word should have been obvious.

Dan sighed. Brown knew nothing about the area or about swamps. There was no telling how deep that water was, how long it went on, or where it would take them. He had led them into the swamp, and instead of leading them out, he was going to lead them even deeper. Then again, Dan had to admit the swamp had come from out of nowhere. One second they were on completely dry land, and literally the next they were in a swamp. He supposed it was just the weird geography of this so-called "new world."

"No need to tarry, men. Who wants to bravely lead the way?" Brown asked, asking for volunteers to step into the ominous swamp waters first.

Benson Huffines, a soldier who had done some medical studies before entering into military service, finally spoke up. "Shouldn't we just head back the way we came? I have a feeling this swamp could be a breeding ground for malaria, if nothing else."

"Nonsense, this isn't India or Africa; these bugs don't carry disease," Alfred said, speaking to Benson as if he were an idiot to suggest such a thing.

Dan sighed again and wondered how the King expected to win the war with feeble-minded leaders like Brown in the field. He thought for a second, trying to figure out the best way to tell Brown they needed to go back the way they had come without insulting him, and ending up with a court-martial.

"Commander, I shall be the one!" Gregory Blake said, hobbling his fat body over to the edge of the water. Everyone in the group, except the Commander, shook their heads. Blake was a total boolicker who would do anything to get in the Commander's good graces. It figured that he would have been in the group that got separated, because Hell itself couldn't have separated his lips from the Commander's backside. Once Blake stepped in, the rest knew their arguments were fruitless and they would soon be knee-deep in stagnant muck.

Blake walked over to the edge of the swamp and prepared to step in, but then stopped. He peered down into the black water as if he had spotted something. "Here now, what's this I see under the—"

Those were the last words he ever spoke, as the next second what appeared to be an impossibly large crocodile sprang from the swamp and enclosed Blake in its jaws, dragging his bloated carcass back under the black water before anyone else could even shout. There was a loud splash and the black water rippled, but both Blake and the monster were gone.

The men all jumped back from the water and within seconds, the sound of musket fire tore through the swamp as the men all fired their guns into the water, hoping to hit what could only have been a creature from Hell that had managed to swallow the biggest man in the group with one gulp.

"Cease fire...cease fire...CEASE FIRE!" the Commander yelled, although by this point the entire group had already emptied their muskets and were reloading, except for Dan. Dan was the most seasoned fighter in the group, and had therefore held his shot until he was certain he had a better target.

"What the blazes was that?" one of the men asked, still aiming his gun into the water with shaky hands.

"I suppose it was a crocodile," Brown said, his voice shaky but still trying to maintain his composure. Dan figured rather than it being bravery, Brown was just too dimwitted to be scared.

"That was unlike any crocodile I've ever seen. Did you see the size of it? And the speed? It came out of nowhere and was gone with him in a second. That's not natural," Dan said.

Dan had been to both India and Africa, and had seen the large crocodiles that infested the rivers there, but he had never seen anything even close to the size of the beast that had just seized Blake. The creature didn't look just like a crocodile—or an alligator, as the ones in the new world were being called. It resembled them both, only more primal and obviously much larger. Dan had a feeling the muskets and pistols they were carrying would be useless against those giant reptiles, and he wondered how many could be in the swamp and moving closer to them right at this very moment.

"We have to get out of here," Dan said, turning to head back down the trail they had used to arrive in the swamp, no longer caring what Commander Brown's orders were. He would rather be alive and on trial than dead and in the belly of a beast.

Dan had taken a few steps when he sunk down to his ankles in muck. He took another step and found himself knee deep in mud. He pulled himself out and moved back, looking over the water and mud that had just appeared behind them.

The other men, including Commander Brown, had turned to follow Dan this time, all of them deciding this swamp was not where they wanted to be. However, they all stared in amazement as water surrounded them on all sides. This was definitely the way they had come in, and it had been bone-dry at the time, but now it was as soggy and wet as the area in front of them.

"Now what the devil is this about?" Dan asked, seeing the mud covering his boots and britches.

"I suppose the tide must have come in while we were waiting here; it's the only explanation that makes sense," Commander Brown said, speaking the first intelligent words most of the men had ever heard coming from his mouth.

They all nodded and muttered among themselves. It had to be the tide. There was no other explanation for this. So why did Dan find that so hard to believe? Dan turned to the swamp again, the dark marsh appearing even more sinister than before. If he didn't know better, he'd think the swamp didn't want them to leave.

"So what do we do now? I am not going into that water," one of the soldiers said, speaking aloud what every man there was already thinking.

"We have to think of something. Give me a minute," Commander Brown said, taking a seat near a tree and rubbing his brow, deep in thought.

Dan glanced up at the trees. There were plenty of them, most of them packed in tight. Live oaks ringed the edge of the swampland, and most of the huge branches on the trees were either touching or nearly touching, each other.

"I think we can climb," Dan said, pointing up at the thick tree limbs. "If we climb these oaks, I think we can travel from branch to branch and stay out of the water. It's risky, but it is safer than staying down here and right now I don't see any choice."

Dan and the entire group turned to Commander Brown, expecting him to veto the suggestion just to exercise his authority. Brown stood and glanced up at the branches, nodding. "Yes, that's just what I was thinking. Let's start climbing men." Brown said, still trying to take credit for the idea. At the moment, however, the men were just relieved they didn't have to mutiny and therefore weren't too concerned over taking credit for ideas.

The large oak they were standing under, had a huge branch that extended out over the water, and the large branch of another oak was only a few feet from it. They could climb out onto the limb and then carefully hop onto the next limb, traveling deeper into the swamp while staying several feet above the black liquid.

As the men lined up to climb, there was another splash, and one more man found himself a victim of the crocodile. He was pulled under and taken even faster than Blake had been. The men weren't sure if it was the same monster that had gotten Blake, but either way they knew they had to move, and fast.

The men shimmied up the tree and across the branch, one after the other. As two of the men made their way out onto the branch together, a loud crack was heard.

"Whoa, men. One at a time on the branches, one at a time," Dan said, not caring at the moment whether Brown would see this as an insult to his authority. Brown said nothing and nodded, the situation showing that he might have possessed at least a small amount of common sense.

The men made their way over as quickly as possible, one at a time on the branches and thankfully the branches held. Once they made it onto the other tree, they had all spread out onto various branches, including some on adjacent trees, waiting there until the next leg of the journey could be planned.

Commander Brown demanded to go across last, showing some military etiquette and also some rare backbone. Dan realized that Brown might not be all bad—he just hadn't faced enough adversity to bring out his good side yet.

Dan made it across and was waiting on the far branch as Commander Brown shimmied his way onto the other branch. As he neared the end of it there was a loud crack and the branch splintered, dropping a few feet down towards the water. The branch held, causing the Commander to slip and now he was holding the branch with both hands, dangling over the black water. Dan made his way to the end of his branch and reached down, trying to grab onto the Commander and pull him up, hoping the branch could support their weight. They were a good fifteen feet out of the water, but considering the size of the monsters they had seen and the fact Brown was hanging down a good ways, he didn't think this position was exactly safe.

"Ay Commander, reach up with one hand and hold on with the other, and I'll pull you on up so you can grab on here," Dan said, holding on with one hand and reaching down with his free one.

"Many thanks, Daniel. When this is all sorted out, I will see to it that you get a promotion out of this," William said as he reached for Dan's hand.

The water below the Commander suddenly erupted in a white froth and the largest shark anyone in the group had ever seen, exploded from the water, swallowing half of the Commander in one gulp as it chomped down on him and dragged him into the black depths of the swamp.

Dan knew he would never forget the expression of shocked horror in the Commander's eyes as the giant fish had dragged him to his death. He scurried back against the tree and leaned against the trunk, shaking at what he had just witnessed.

It was impossible. For one thing, sharks just didn't get that big. They had all heard the sea monster stories spouted by sailors full of too much rum, but no sharks that big had ever been proven to exist. And a shark that large in a *swamp?* There was no way. The crocodiles were one thing—as much of this country was still unexplored—and who knew how big some of the reptiles could get? But the brackish water of this swamp should not have been able to support a fish that size, not to mention the water shouldn't have been deep enough to hide beasts of such proportions. Daniel was a God-fearing man, and had never believed in witchcraft. But one thing he was now sure of: this swamp was cursed, and they needed to get out *now.*

The men all began to scramble along the tree branches, moving from tree to tree quite easily. The oaks were growing right out of the swamp, just like the cypress. This was unusual but none of the soldiers knew enough about trees to comment. As they crawled along, it began to get darker and darker in the swamp and they all knew it would soon be night. None of the men had lanterns and there would be no practical way of starting a fire in the trees. Soon it would be pitch black, as the canopy was too dense to allow much through in the way of moonlight.

As the men made their way along the branches, one of them, a Yorkshire man by the name of Archie Harrison, slipped and fell with a cry. The men all watched in horror as he tumbled towards the black water, but he stopped in mid-air a few feet under the branch. They squinted in the half-light, wondering what had stopped him, and they were able to make out what appeared to be some netting that had broken his fall. They were all unsure as to who could have placed a net in the middle of such a horrible place, but they assumed it was perhaps some

Indians who had left a fishing net out, or maybe even a net to catch some birds.

The men were all pondering a way to rescue their comrade when they noticed he was squirming and frozen in place. "Hey now, this thing is sticky as molasses. What the hell is all over it?" Archie asked as he struggled, the netting fixed tight to his uniform. His musket was also held fast and try as he might Archie couldn't budge it.

"Just stay tight a bit Archie, we'll think of something," Dan called down.

Suddenly, a giant spider the size of a large dog scuttled onto the web and latched onto Archie, sinking its fangs into his shoulder before he even had a chance to react. The spider appeared to be a type of Black Widow, as it was jet black with the same body type. However, this spider had bright stripes of various colors running all over its back. Stripes of bright red, blue, yellow, green, aqua, gray and several other colors encircled the monster, making it beautiful in a grotesque way. The men watched frozen as the spider began to weave its web with its long spindly legs, slowly cocooning Archie up like a mummy.

"Oh God, it burns! It burns like fire!" Archie screamed as he fought to get free, his body held in place by the sticky web. The spider hung onto Archie obscenely as it injected him with venom which no doubt was meant to liquefy his innards and turn him into a meal.

The men were at first frozen with revulsion, but as Archie's screams grew more and more high-pitched they acted and opened fire on the vile arachnid. Several of the musket balls struck the creature, tearing off chunks of it and amputating one of its legs. Archie's screams had already turned into low moans as the spider turned its attention to the men up in the tree above it.

The men drew their pistols and prepared to fire again as the spider hissed and leaped at them. One of the men acted quickly and impaled the spider on his bayonet as it leapt, the spider wriggling as it dangled on the end of the gun. The soldier dropped his musket as the spider's legs slapped at him, the weight of the gun pulling the spider down as it plopped into the water with a slight splash. The men all held their pistols at the ready, waiting for the spider to reappear. It never did. Whether it had drowned or something in the water had gotten it, the men would never know, nor did they care, as long as it was gone.

Dan stared at Archie. It was very dark by now, and Daniel wasn't sure if it was a trick of the shadows or not, but he could swear Archie was withered, his skin wrinkled like parchment. He was still making very weak moaning sounds, but it was quite obvious there was nothing they could do for him.

Dan decided to make an executive decision as he reloaded his musket, thankful that the damp air of the swamp hadn't permeated it with enough moisture to make it unusable. He took careful aim at Archie's forehead, barely able to make it out in the gloom.

"Sorry, you poor devil, but the best I can do now is put you out of your misery." Dan said as he fired, the musket ball striking Archie in the forehead and killing him instantly. The only sound the bullet made when it smashed into his head was a dull smack, like the sound one would hear if a bullet were to penetrate a piece of paper. The spider had potent venom indeed, and Dan prayed he'd never encounter another in his lifetime.

By now it was pitch black, but the men still struggled along the branches further, none of them wanting to be near the giant web any longer, lest the spider's mate came calling. Several of the men had close calls, almost slipping, but always managing to stay aloft, usually with the help of a friend.

As they made it to an exceptionally large oak, Dan called out a suggestion. "Here now, this tree is large and has several branches. I say we stay here for the night and continue on at first light. We can sleep in shifts and maybe we might live to see the morning."

Some of the men agreed but several of them protested and kept moving, fear getting the better of their intellect. Only a handful of men ended up staying with Dan, and they all agreed to sleep in shifts. As it happened, no one got any sleep.

All through the night, the sounds of men screaming could be heard as the soldiers who had decided to travel on, met their ends in various gruesome ways. The soldiers with Dan all lay flat on the branches with their muskets gripped in sweaty hands as they waited out the dark. Along with the sounds of dying men, the night was also filled with other sounds—growls, screams, hisses and other noises, sounds which were not made by any beast with which they were familiar. This swamp was truly a parcel of Hell.

Although he never went into deep slumber, Dan did drift in and out of consciousness through the night. He was lost in a fever dream all night, as fear exhausted his body and mind, but didn't give him any rest to ease his fatigue. Finally, after the worst night of his life, daylight began to break though the trees.

Dan cautiously examined the nearby branches, his musket ready to fire. He saw nothing out of the ordinary. Only three other men had remained in the tree with Dan, and there was no sign of any of the others. The four men didn't bother to speak, but instead began to carefully make their way along the branches.

The men were tired, sweaty, and covered in insect bites, but still happy to be alive. Horror had made them numb, which served to benefit them in their travel. After several hours of moving through the trees, with the men eating nothing and taking small sips of water from their canteens, they finally came upon what appeared to be dry land.

They all climbed onto the branches over the ground, wondering if their eyes could be deceiving them. Dan broke a piece off of his branch and tossed it to the ground, testing for both the firmness of the soil as well as the presence of any nearby monsters. The stick bounced on the apparently hard bank, and nothing appeared, so the men figured it must be safe.

Carefully, they shimmied down the tree, staying as far from the water's edge as possible, before they all gathered in the clearing, taking a seat to catch their breath. They all stared at one another, still not speaking. It was as if their minds had shut down and their bodies were moving automatically. Nature had put them into survival mode, and that might be the only way they would get out of this hellhole alive.

Dan stood up and the others followed his lead, standing as well. He surveyed the area and decided the best direction was *away* from the water, so he began to head down the clearest area in the thick overgrown forest.

Before they had taken two steps, there was a thunderous growl and a huge, furry, humanoid creature bounded from the woods, grabbing one of the men by the legs and snatching him into the air. As the other three men backed away in terror, the monster roared and slammed his capture into a tree, the sound of his skull shattering and spine snapping audible as the creature slammed him against the tree repeatedly, beating him to death as he swung the grown man's body like it was a small child.

The creature was eight feet tall and looked like a giant hairy man. Its face was covered in fur and appeared to be simian, but it was hard to see its features due to the thick brown fur that covered its entire frame. The men didn't know it, but this was a Sasquatch, and it was hungry for human flesh. Once the body went limp the monster let it fall to ground, still keeping a tight grip on the legs as it turned and growled again at the remaining three men, daring them to try to take his kill.

Dan reacted first, firing his musket and striking the creature in the shoulder. The bullet tore a bloody hole in the fur, and the other two men fired soon after, both shots striking the creature in the chest, staggering it but not dropping it. The creature kept its grip on the body and roared a challenge at them.

The beast was more concerned with keeping its kill rather than making another, so the three men took off running, being sure to keep their pistols at hand as they tore off into the woods.

All three men ran as if Satan himself were upon their heels, but there was no pursuit from the monster as they crashed through the swamp. They were stepping in muck that came over their ankles as they ran, but so far had not come across any huge bodies of water. The three men just kept running, not gauging direction anymore, just forward.

Dan eventually began to tire, and one of the men passed him, now running ahead of Dan who had been leading the pack. Dan tried to mouth a warning to him to be careful, but he was so out of breath he couldn't form the words. There was a loud *whooosh* and the man ahead of Dan disappeared in a huge mound of vegetation. Dan stopped running and stepped back, trying to understand what had just happened.

It seemed a giant plant had just swallowed him. Dan could hear screams coming from inside the green pod that now blocked his way, and it sounded as if the man were being eaten alive. Dan drew his saber and slashed at the plant, hacking at it with abandon. The other soldier had come up on him by now, and he had drawn his saber too. The two of them managed to slash the pod open, and they stepped back as a foul smelling liquid came rushing from the opened plant. Their companion also fell from the plant, no longer screaming. He was now not much more than a skeleton with bits of hair and flesh attached. The giant man-eating plant had managed to dissolve all of his clothing and most of his flesh in just seconds.

Dan and the other soldier began to run yet again, carefully moving around the huge plant. They both knew they could be killed at any second, but at this point they had no other options. The idea of a slow and cautious walk through this haunted forest was out of the question.

They both ran for hours, stopping to walk as needed before running again once they had their breath. Their uniforms were ripped and torn to tatters and their skin was also shredded as they made their way through the swamp. They had not seen any other monsters, but they had heard things near them as they ran. The swamp had to end soon; how big could it be?

They continued running until the sun went down yet again, both of them nearing exhaustion. Could it really be time for night again already, or did time just pass differently in this damned swamp? They weren't sure.

As the moon rose in the sky, moonlight filtered down upon them as they hurried along. The woods weren't nearly as thick in this area, so the moonlight lit the area up well. Then the howling began. Both men stopped and gripped their guns tightly as the howl of the wolf filled their ears. It was so loud it hurt, echoing in their skulls and driving them dizzy with its volume. They once again tore off running.

Daniel gradually pulled ahead. He was fitter than his companion and therefore ran faster. The howling continued and was getting closer and closer. Something crashed through the woods behind them, and even though he kept running Dan turned his head at the sound. He was rewarded with the grisly sight of his last companion being tackled to the ground by a gray form that was something between a wolf and a man—a werewolf. The man barely had time to yelp as the werewolf buried its snout in his throat. Dan turned away and ran faster, the gurgling sound of the man and the slurping sounds of sloppy eating, following him.

Dan kept going faster, stumbling and falling, rising and running again. Then Dan found himself in a clearing. It came upon him so suddenly he hadn't even had time to stop running when his shins connected with something hard, bloodying them and sending him down right on his face. He stood up, barely able to rise due to the bruising of his legs, and turned around trying to see what had tripped him. It was a headstone. He perused his surroundings, and found himself in the middle of a graveyard.

Dan began to cry with joy, elated to have found his way out of the swamp. No one would put a graveyard in a swamp—he had to be on the edge. He stopped and tried to catch his breath, still too near the woods to be comfortable.

He turned and carefully made his way through the headstones when he suddenly halted. There was someone in the graveyard. The man was still several yards away, but no doubt this was a human being and not some bloodthirsty beast. He got closer and saw a very nicely dressed man at one of the graves. He was very tall, over six feet, and thin. He appeared to be very pale, although that could have just been the moonlight.

"Sir? Can I trouble you for a moment?" Daniel asked, at this point not caring if this person was on his side or not. He would gladly surrender if it meant a way out of here. "I was lost in the swamp, can I ask a favor?"

The man turned and smiled as Dan approached, and Dan only had time to see the bright glowing red eyes and the long white fangs before the man pounced on him. And then Daniel saw nothing at all.

The regiment was never seen again, and all members were assumed to have been killed in battle.

TWO

Savannah, Georgia. Present.

Shade Channing was awake before the alarm clock went off. To say he had trouble sleeping since coming home from Afghanistan would be an understatement. The change in time zone and environment alone had been bad enough, but with the added Post Traumatic Stress Disorder on top of everything else, he had had many sleepless nights. He stood up and stretched, his body still lean and muscular from his time in the service. Shade, as a former member of SEAL Team 6, had served more than a few tours in the Middle East. That was then. Now, he had stepped away to pursue other interests. It had been recommended he retire from military service due to stress-related reasons. It was all just getting to be too much for him, and he knew it, so he took the advice of the military doctors and opted out.

He took a moment to examine himself in the mirror as he stood there in his boxers. He stood at six foot three and weighed a solid two hundred and forty pounds. He was still in great shape at the age of thirty-five, and he was in better shape than most men half his age. The SEAL-training regimen was something he planned to follow throughout the rest of his life. He had no intention of growing soft and fat. His jet-black hair was still cut in the short military-style he was accustomed to and he could still burn holes in a person with the cold stare of his steel gray eyes. He had one tattoo, a skull on his right arm. He didn't get a trident or any of the other mythically popular tattoos SEALs supposedly have. He wouldn't have a tattoo at all, but too much partying can lead to crazy things.

Shade also had a few scars on his body, most notably a long thin scar across his left shoulder he had gotten on his last mission caused by shrapnel from an IED, an explosive device. He had lost a few friends in that mission, and he had no problem with it being his last. He wished he could erase it from his memory, but he knew he'd never forget.

Shade glanced at the digital clock on his nightstand and saw it was getting late. He had a nine a.m job interview and it was already five past seven.. The traffic in Savannah wasn't terrible, but he also wasn't sure exactly where he was going and only had some hastily- scrawled directions to the interview location. He had tried to find a driving map on the internet but for some reason had had no luck—it was like the address didn't exist. He had the same issue with his GPS. But considering he had found his way through the desert in Iraq with not much more than a compass, he thought he could find one little Department of Natural Resources office.

Shade undressed, climbed into the shower, and turned the water on—cold only. He closed his eyes and stood under the icy stream as he tried to concentrate on his day. Before he had joined the military, Shade had plans of being a game warden, and had gone to college on the GI Bill with a double major of environmental science and law enforcement. He got his degrees, but found military service suited him and he pursued a career with the Navy, eventually ending up as one of the very best, a member of SEAL Team Six. But now that he was ready to put the military behind him, he was ready to pursue his first love and try to get a job as a game warden. His family had always had a love of the outdoors, and supposedly some of the relatives from before his time had been game wardens themselves.

He had surfed several websites attempting to find jobs with the Georgia DNR, the Department of Natural Resources, and had submitted his application. He finally got a response, but was confused when the saw the position was for an area of the state called Black Swamp. He had heard of Black Swamp, it was located not too far from the city of Jesup, but this Black Swamp was supposedly right near Savannah and from the directions he had received from his phone conversation with the DNR Commissioner, this swamp was not the same one.

He finished his shower and stepped out, drying off and hurrying to get dressed. He was told not to dress up because they would be touring the swamp, so he put on some hiking boots, khaki pants and a forest green long sleeved button-down shirt. It was September, but most likely the mosquitoes would still be out, so he wanted to cover as much skin as possible. He also put on his NAVY baseball cap, not wanting the sun or the bugs on his head.

Shade pondered his life as he drove. No wife, no kids. A long line of girlfriends, but his career had left him no room for anything serious. He was currently living in a rented apartment in the suburbs of Savannah, a one-bedroom apartment that was nice enough but nothing spectacular. It fit his needs. After sleeping on rocks in the mountains in freezing temperatures, it was a palace to him.

Shade climbed into his brand new Chevrolet Tahoe SUV and started it up, checking his watch and seeing it was just after 8. He pulled the tungsten metallic-colored vehicle into traffic and headed towards Savannah, keeping the handwritten directions nearby. Shade had grown up in Savannah and knew the streets, so it didn't take him long to reach the general area of the interview, but he had no clue exactly where to go from there. The swamp was of course not right in the city limits, but just outside. Shade found himself on a very old and deserted stretch of road, with nothing much but woods on either side. As he drove along past miles and miles of pine trees, he wondered if he had made a wrong turn. Suddenly he passed by a small break in the woods, which was barely visible. Thankfully there was no traffic around, so he turned the SUV around in the middle of the road and drove back. It was indeed a road, although to call it that would be a stretch. It was a dirt road with little maintenance and it lead into thick woods. This had to be the place. Shade shrugged and pulled onto the road, glad he had chosen the optional four wheel drive for his vehicle because he had a feeling he might need it.

The road was even bumpier than it first appeared, and Shade found himself experiencing a rough ride as he made his way down it. The road wasn't big enough for two-way traffic, so Shade hoped he didn't pass anyone coming from the opposite direction. After he drove along for what felt like several miles but was just a few, the road finally ended. Shade saw the game warden office, a fairly nice log cabin that was situated right on the edge of the swamp. A decent-sized dock was right beside the cabin, and had two boats tethered: a large twenty foot fiberglass boat and a smaller twelve foot metal boat. There was also a fairly large shed out back, made of treated plywood with a tin roof.

A game warden SUV was parked near the office as well as an older model, dark blue pickup truck which also had the game warden seal on its doors. Shade pulled into the lot beside the pickup and got out, taking a look around before he went to the office.

As expected, it was already hot and humid even at this early hour, and the mosquitoes and gnats were already buzzing. Shade wondered why he had never heard of this swamp. He used to do a fair amount of hunting and fishing and knew several people that were obsessed with it, but still he had never heard of this swamp nor had any idea it even existed.

He shrugged and walked out onto the dock, surveying the area. It could have been any typical swamp. It had a lot of trees —mostly cypress—and other vegetation, and the water was pitch black. It had the odd smell swamp water carries, but nothing he saw surprised him. It felt nice and peaceful, something Shade had been looking forward to experiencing. He could definitely see himself serving here as a game warden.

"Hello there, I guess you must be my interview," a voice spoke from behind Shade, startling him slightly. He turned to see an older Native American man standing behind him. He was fairly tall, just over six feet, and appeared lean and wiry. He had his long white hair braided into double braids that ran down past his chest. He was dressed in khaki pants and a camouflage long sleeved shirt, and had on high leather moccasin boots. He wasn't wearing an official uniform; he was wearing a utility belt with handcuffs and a sidearm that appeared to be a 9mm semi-auto.

"Oh, sorry, yes I am. I'm Shade, Shade Channing," Shade said, reaching his hand out for a shake. *How the hell had this old man managed to sneak up on me like that?*

The old man smiled and shook Shade's hand firmly, his grip showing surprising strength. "I am Waya Firehat. Waya means wolf in Cherokee, Firehat is just some goofy name a white man gave my family years ago. My Cherokee name is hard to pronounce but basically translates to *head on fire*, so we got stuck with Firehat. I think I had a relative that had married an Irishman and ended up with red hair. Sorry if I sound like I'm rambling, but I like to get the Firehat story out of the way right up front."

Shade returned the smile, "It's nice to meet you. Are you the current game warden here?"

"Alas, no, the game warden that worked here was killed in an unfortunate accident. His name was Adahy Firehat. He was my son." Waya bowed his head and cleared his throat.

"Oh, I am so sorry to hear that, I didn't know. What happened?" Shade asked.

"As I said, it was an accident. In any case, let's go inside so we can start the process," Waya waved Shade on as he walked towards the office. Shade followed along and entered the building behind him. It was nice inside of the cabin. Hardwood floors along with the requisite mounted animals on display around the office. There were several Deer heads, various fish, a bobcat and even a large alligator under a glass case that dominated the lobby. It must have been fifteen feet long and the taxidermist had done such a great job on it that it appeared to still be alive.

"Damn, that's a big ass gator," Shade said, stepping over to the case to admire it.

"Ah yes, old Lucifer. He used to live out in the bay there until he died of old age back in the seventies. He was over a hundred years old when he finally kicked." Waya explained.

"Back in the seventies? How long has this office been around?"

"Oh it was opened back in the late 1700s. This was one of the first game warden stations in the state."

"You're kidding me? I've never even heard of it until recently."

"Not many have. It's of a well-kept secret," Waya said as he took a seat behind the desk. "Have a seat, Shade," he said, waving to one of the two large leather chairs that faced the desk. Shade took a seat as Waya began to flip through some paperwork, presumably Shade's resume and the online application he had completed earlier.

"I didn't think to bring any paperwork with me, I'm a little out of touch with job interviews, but I did email everything I had and I completed the online application. I sent my resume, some letters of recommendation--"

"Yes, no worries, I have it all right here," Waya said,

saving Shade any further speech. Shade sat quietly as Waya shuffled through the papers. "I have already reviewed it, but I thought I'd take another look to see if I have any questions while you're in front of me."

"Absolutely, take your time," Shade said, glancing around the office. There was a large aquarium at the other end of the room. It was a fifty-gallon tank, and he could see large-mouth bass, bream, and other local freshwater fish inside. He had to admit, the office was impressive. He found himself wanting the job now. He had forgotten how much he had been in love with the idea of being a game warden, but it was returning to him.

"Navy SEAL huh? And you have the prior experience. All right, I think you'll do," Waya said, closing the file and standing up.

Shade stood up as well, slightly confused. "Do you mean I have the job?"

Waya nodded. "Yep, it's yours, congratulations. You are the new Game Warden of Black Swamp."

Shade grinned and reached out to shake Waya's hand again. "Thanks! That was the easiest interview I've ever had in my life!"

Waya pumped his hand vigorously a few times. "I kind of knew as soon as I saw your paperwork that you'd be the one. Now, it's time for orientation. This may take a while, but it's all very important."

Waya stood up and pulled a thick three ring binder from a bookshelf behind the desk. "In all honesty, everything you need to know is in this notebook. How to use the computer, run license and registration checks, issue licenses and registrations, pretty much everything is right here. I will let you look over it on your own since I would only confuse you. If you have questions, let me know and either I'll answer them or point you to the people that can."

Shade nodded, "Sounds good to me."

"Now, for the next step, let me show you around the office." Waya stood and walked to the nearest door. There were two doors in the office in addition to the front door. Waya opened the door. "This is the living quarters. Now you won't be expected to be a resident here, but there are times when you will find it handy to have an apartment you can use nearby. It's got a bed, bathroom with a shower, kitchenette, pretty much anything you'd need."

Shade peeked in the doorway as Waya flipped the light switch one. It was a pretty standard living area with a full-sized bed. Nothing fancy, but still better than any of the barracks. He could deal with this easily.

Waya flipped the lights off and closed the door, moving to the next one. "This is a very important room, this is the armory," he said before he opened the door. It was a decent-sized room, about as big as the main lobby, and there was a gun cabinet on the back of the wall, along with what appeared to be gun lockers and a gun safe on opposite walls as well. *How many guns does a game warden office need?*

Waya walked back to the desk and opened a drawer, pulling out a ring of keys and then stepping back into the room, waving Shade in after him. "Here are your standard guns." Waya unlocked the cabinet and opened it, presenting Shade with an assortment of typical long guns. There were a few pump-action shotguns, a bolt action .30-06 rifle with a scope, a .30-30 lever action rifle and even a couple of automatic shotguns. It seemed like a lot of guns for a small game warden office. Waya opened the drawers at the bottom of the case and Shade saw several handguns, including one in a holster and belt which Waya handed to him. "Here, that's your service weapon. It's a 9mm semi-automatic with which I'm sure you're familiar." Shade saw a few additional handguns similar to his own, and also a few revolvers in the drawers too. There were also boxes and boxes of ammunition for all of the various caliber guns in the cabinet.

"Damn, man, are you expecting a war?" Shade said with a smile as he tried the belt on, wanting to get used to wearing it as soon as possible.

Waya smiled weakly, "Something like that. By the way, make sure you write your sizes down for me before you go, we want to get you into a uniform as quickly as possible."

Shade nodded, "Sure thing."

As Shade adjusted the belt Waya watched him silently. "Shade, describe in your own words what a game warden's job is to you."

Shade finished his belt and looked at Waya. "I guess it's just what it sounds like—protecting the game. I have to be sure everyone's following hunting and fishing laws, make sure they have the correct permits, make sure they aren't using illegal tactics. All of that. And I guess also keeping an eye out on the animals and fish, watching for anything unusual. Sicknesses, invasive species, anything out of the ordinary. I think it's mostly just riding around in a boat and writing tickets, isn't it?" Shade winked.

Waya once again smiled. "We normally try to break new game wardens in slowly here, but with your background I think I need to go ahead and let you know what you're getting into. Come with me."

Shade wasn't sure exactly what Waya was talking about as he followed him back out into the office. Waya took the key ring and unlocked one of the bottom drawers on the desk, taking out what appeared to be a very thick and very old photo album, which he set on the desk between them. "How open-minded are you?"

Shade blinked. "I'm pretty open minded, but if you are going to show me some kinda weird sex pictures I'm afraid I'll have to let you know upfront I find that unsettling," Shade said, smiling and winking to let Waya know he was joking.

Waya once again met Shade with a weak smile. "No sex pictures, but something much more disturbing." He slid the photo album over in front of Shade turning it around to face him. "Open it up, and tell me what you see."

Shade watched as Waya opened up the worn leather album, looking down at the first picture. It was an antique photo, one of the oldest Shade had even seen. It showed several men standing around what appeared to be an alligator the size of a dinosaur. Shade had seen huge saltwater crocodiles during his travels around the world, but nothing like this. There were ten men in the picture, wearing coveralls and dungarees and other vintage clothing, all standing in a row behind the gator—they weren't even shoulder-to-shoulder and they still didn't reach the length of the monster's body. Shade could only guess, but it appeared to be over thirty feet long and from the thickness of its body, Shade would say it weighed at least a ton. The only writing on the picture was a small date written in the bottom right hand corner: 1881.

Shade stared at Waya, "Is this supposed to be real? Is this

is a joke or what?"

Waya shook his head, "Keep looking."

Shade flipped the brittle page, this time seeing several photographs on the two pages now facing him. They all appeared to be just as old as the first photo. He glanced at each picture and saw several unusual sights. One picture showed two men standing around what appeared to be an enormous Great White Shark which was hanging by its tail. The fish was so huge it didn't even fit into the photo.

Another picture showed what could only be called a giant snake. There was a man in the picture to give it some perspective, but it still had to be off. The snake was thicker than the man and coiled. The snake's head was bigger than the man's body, and the head was also diamond shaped, indicating a venomous reptile. Not even the largest constrictors grew that large, much less the smaller vipers.

Yet another photo showed what had to be a giant rat, once again bigger than a man. Shade flipped through the photo book. The pictures became more recent as he flipped through, each one still marked with a year. As he browsed through the early 1900s, Shade saw such impossible things as giant wasps, an ape-like creature that could be Bigfoot, and there was even one of a fish-man monster from a fifties horror movie.

He flipped through the decades, the thirties, forties, fifties, and the pictures just got even more bizarre. Insects of impossible sizes filled several photos, along with humanoid shaped creatures. He closed the book and pushed it back towards Waya.

"Are you screwing with me? Is this some kind of screw with the new guy thing? What the hell is going on? This is a joke right?" he asked, for some reason the absurdity of the situation pissing him off now.

"Those pictures are all real, and everything you saw in it came from this swamp." Waya said without cracking a smile.

"Damn it, I've been to Iraq, Afghanistan, and a bunch of countries you probably haven't heard of, and I've killed a lot of people. I don't need this bullshit from you!" Shade stood up and found himself shaking, his Post Traumatic Stress Disorder triggered by this latest turn of events.

"Shade, please sit down. I need to tell you some things,

and it's best if you calm down before we talk. Do you need anything to drink, some water, maybe a beer?" Waya asked, standing.

Shade tried to calm himself. "Yeah, I could drink a beer," he said, sitting back down and gripping the arms of the chair to try to control his emotions.

Waya nodded and walked into the apartment, coming back with two bottles of imported beer. He took a bottle opener from the desk and opened both of them, handing one to Shade. Shade took it and gulped down half of it in one swallow as Waya took conservative sips of his own.

"This swamp isn't a regular swamp," Waya said.

Shade said nothing, just glared at him from his chair. "So you are trying to tell me everything in those pictures is real? What's going on? Cut the shit here."

"Everything is real, and there's so much more that's not in the pictures. This swamp, it's a cursed place, a haunted place. I'm Cherokee, and my people have always spoken of this land as cursed. Half the time you can't even find it, like it's not really here."

Shade sat up. "What are you saying?"

"Let me ask you, you've lived around here your entire life, correct? And I'm sure from your background you and your buddies have done plenty of hunting, fishing, and camping—am I right?"

Shade nodded but didn't speak.

"All right then, and have you ever heard of this place? Ever seen it? Has anyone you know ever heard of it?"

Shade shook his head quietly.

"See what I mean? It's always been here, probably forever. I know the legends go back before there even was a Cherokee Nation. And yet nobody sees it, nobody knows it's here. That's because sometimes it is, sometimes it isn't. Maybe only certain people can find it—I don't know, nothing's ever been proven. There are stories of people wandering into it from time to time, but no one knows how or why." Waya paused to let this sink in as he watched Shade staring at him, his expression not giving away his thoughts.

Shade took another gulp of beer, "Keep talking."

"That's how I knew you were the right one for the job.

You're the only applicant that can even find the damn place! The ad has been up for months, we've got calls, but nobody can ever find us. We have to make up some bullshit excuse about the position being filled and give them another office address if they get pushy. I don't know why, but you're the only choice for the job," Waya said, watching Shade for a reaction.

Shade finished his beer in one final gulp and sat the bottle down on the edge of the desk. "So what you're telling me is I'd be the game warden of what, a haunted swamp? A swamp full of monsters? This is ridiculous, I think I better pass." Shade stood up and began to remove his gun belt

"You can save a lot of lives if you take the job," Waya said.

Shade stopped and just stared at him, "What the hell are you talking about?"

"Shade, the, well, the monsters, sometimes they get out. The swamp needs a game warden to make sure they don't. People die all the time because of this swamp, it just gets covered up or explained another way," Waya said.

Shade sat back down. "Talk fast, what are you saying?"

Waya spoke, "The job of the game warden is to stop the bad things from getting out of the swamp. You can't stop them all, but without someone here there's no telling what could get through, the world could be in danger."

Shade shook his head. "I've spent years now with people telling me the damn world was in danger, I doubted it when the brass told me, and I doubt it even more now. Why don't you just stop them? Aren't you a game warden here, too? Why do you need me?"

Waya stared at his desk as he spoke, "I used to be the game warden here, but I got too old for the job. I'm just an assistant now. My son was the game warden and he...Well, he died stopping something that could have been a catastrophe for mankind."

Shade glared at Waya, "What the hell do you mean? Spit it out and stop beating around the damn bush."

Waya sat up, serious now as he was getting sick of Shade's bitching, "Listen, do you remember that hurricane that popped up here a few months back? The one that came out of nowhere and no one could explain? Sorta tore the coastline up, but for some reason the radar and satellite images were all fuzzy?"

Shade did remember hearing about that, it had happened right before he got home. "Yeah, so?"

"That wasn't a hurricane, it was a damned monster! Something tried to get through, something big. I mean real Lovecraft elder gods shit. My son managed to stop it, but he died in the attempt. Now as far as we know, something like that is rare, but we don't know how many times it's happened in the past, or if it will happen again. But if that thing had made it out of the swamp, who knows what could have happened."

"So what you're saying is you're offering me the chance to die for eighteen bucks an hour and benefits? Shit, how the hell can I refuse that?" Shade said sarcastically.

Waya sighed, "Listen, the thing is there's some scary shit out there and we need a bad-ass son of a bitch to take care of it. And my friend, you may be an asshole or you may not be, but one thing you are is a bad-ass son of a bitch. If anyone can stop the things in this swamp, you can."

This time it was Shade's turn to sigh. "I can't believe I'm having this discussion with you. I used to read some horror books back in high school, EC Comics, shit like that. And I've seen all the shitty horror movies, but this? I dunno, man, this is heavy."

"Listen, at least give it a shot, if things don't work out, fine, you can leave and we'll just have to deal with it, but please give it a shot. You are here for a reason, I don't know why, but the game wardens that make it here are always the right ones. I guess maybe some good is in place to help us deal with the bad, shit, I don't know." Waya shut his eyes and rubbed them with both palms as Shade watched him.

"Yeah the problem being, if things don't work out I could end up dead. Not exactly the best terms to leave a job," Shade said, half smiling now.

Waya stopped rubbing his eyes and looked at Shade, happy to see a smile. "Will you at least let me show you around and see how things suit you? It's not quite as bad as I make it sound."

Monsters everywhere you turn and it's not as bad as it sounds? Shade shrugged, "You know, it's not like I haven't thought about putting a gun in my mouth and ending this shit anyway, so if suicide by monster can be an option, I'm open to it. Tell me more."

Waya examined Shade, trying to gauge how seriously to take his comment. "Most of the time this will be a quiet job. You just ride around in the boat and maybe walk around in the dry parts of the swamp some. Most of the wildlife is typical. Just catalog it, keep an eye out, just like you would anywhere else. From time to time, people do wander in trying to hunt and fish. We don't know how or why, it's random, but it does happen. If so, check their licenses and registration. If anything is the least bit off, send them out. If it checks out good, make up an excuse and send them off. Either way, get them the hell out of here. And always send them by the main road. If you find them deeper in the swamp, lead them out until you get back here. Do not let them try to find their own way out, they'll never make it."

Shade listened to everything Waya said, but was still finding it hard to believe. It sounded like something out of a science fiction movie, not real life. "All right, get everybody the hell out of here. Check."

"Oh and one other thing," Waya opened the desk and took out a badge and a wallet, which he opened on the desk to reveal a second badge. "Always keep a badge with you. It's best to wear this one and keep the wallet in your pocket as a backup. This swamp can do strange things; it's easy to get lost out there. These badges are your totems, with these you won't get lost."

Shade was skeptical. "It's good to know the swamp has such respect for authority."

Waya shook his head, "Yeah, yeah, it's nothing like that. I have, let's say, *prepared* these badges for you, so they will act as totems. Don't go into the swamp without them, and don't lose them. A few game wardens have, and they were all replaced pretty quickly."

Shade examined the badges, "You do some kinda witch doctor shit on these?"

Waya nodded and smiled, "Yeah, heap big witch doctor shit."

This time it was Shade's turn to shake his head, "You probably don't even work here, do you? I bet the real game warden's body is in the back room and you're some crazy ass Indian that wandered up here to kill and rape me as soon as you get the chance, in that order."

Waya laughed again, "I won't kill you."

Shade laughed too, and added "Or rape me either I hope."

Waya sized him up. "I don't know. You're pretty hot for a white boy."

Shade flipped Waya the double bird.

"All right, all kidding aside, I need to get down to the serious shit with you. When you run into the bad shit, the monsters, you kill them. That's it, no questions asked. Kill them and just leave the carcasses where they lay, the swamp will take care of the rest. This isn't tag and release we're talking, you show no mercy and you take these things out." Waya said, all trace of humor gone from his voice as he gave Shade a severe look.

"Game warden here really means killing the game, I got it," Shade said, surprised at how easily he was accepting this situation.

"Now come with me, and I'll show you how you go about killing these things," Waya said as he lead Shade back into the armory, Shade following along.

"This explains why you have so many guns and ammo here, but honestly for some of that shit in the pictures these guns just don't look like they'll cut it," Shade said, watching as Waya used the key ring he had brought along to unlock the large locker.

Shade's jaw dropped when the locker was opened. The weapon cache inside rivaled any of the weapon arrays he had seen throughout his entire military career. Sub-machine guns, assault rifles and combat shotguns lined the interior. Big caliber handguns lined the bottom. There was also grenade launchers, some of them mounted underneath the machine guns. There was even some heavy artillery including Rocket Propelled Grenades, Anti-Tank Rockets, hand grenades and a flame thrower. Clips of ammo also lined the locker. It was a survivalists' wet dream.

Shade whistled as he examined the locker. "Ho-ly shit, now this is what I call an armory!" Shade had always been a weapon enthusiast, and he had to admit this was like being a kid gifted with an entire toy box full of new toys.

Waya nodded, the reaction as he had expected, "I thought you might like this locker."

Shade began to take some of the guns down, checking them over and being very pleased with what he was seeing.

These were high-dollar guns, and they were in great condition. "Now how the hell does a game warden get the funds for weaponry like this?" Shade asked as he sighted down an M16 with an M203 Grenade Launcher attached.

"Ah, I'm glad you asked. The government knows about this place. It's like area 51, but real. I mean, this may look like a lot of money, but when you compare it to the cost of a jet or a destroyer, it's change. They just skim a little off the top of some other programs and slide the extra into our budget, much like all of the other black ops programs the government runs under the table," Waya explained.

Shade nodded as he knew exactly what Waya meant. He himself had been a part of some of those secretly funded black ops missions. Shade put the gun back in and stepped back, still looking over the firearms wide-eyed. "Not to get too greedy here, but what's in that last locker?" Shade asked, indicating the slightly smaller gun safe in the room.

"This one is the special stuff," Waya said, taking another key from the ring and opening the final surprise in the room.

This time Shade was just shocked. This locker was filled with several strange weapons, but they were things Shade knew about. Wooden stakes, several machetes, what appeared to be bottles of chemicals, and a lot of silver-bladed weapons. There were also several bullets and clips of various sizes. Shade picked one up, popping a bullet out for inspection. "Silver," he said, more to himself then Waya.

"Yes, this is what we call the special locker. Certain things in the swamp can only be killed certain ways, and we've worked hard over the years to try to stock those things." Waya said, picking up a wooden stake about three feet long and testing the sharpness of the tip with his thumb. "The lucky part is most them can be killed with silver. It's like monster poison. Rule of thumb, if you aren't sure, use silver."

Shade browsed the weapons, noticing some of the blades had inscriptions and a few also appeared to be made of other metals such as iron. Waya watched Shade's eyes. "Sometimes you may run into something that may take some thought, but hopefully you'll be able to get your hands on it when you need it."

Shade turned to Waya. "This is fucking nuts."

"Yep, that's a good way to describe it. So are you ready to go into the swamp yet?" Waya asked as he took a clip of 9mm silver bullets from the safe and then locked it, handing the clip to Shade, "You better hang onto these, you may need them. I'm already covered," he said, patting his sidearm to indicate it was already loaded with silver.

Shade took the clip and stared at it like he'd been handed a live snake, the whole situation hard to fathom. He stuck the clip in his pocket and followed Waya out of the room.

Waya walked out onto the dock and headed over to the bigger boat. "Always use this boat for your patrols unless for some reason the water is really shallow or you know you'll be going down a smaller channel. It's better to stay in the big boat as much as you can."

Shade had seen the things in the pictures, everything from giant sharks and gators to huge alligator snapping turtles. He had a feeling he'd definitely be in the big boat as much as possible.

Waya walked to the back of the boat and lifted the seat, taking out a large tackle box. "Always keep this tackle box full, it may save your life sometime. There's also a spare in the apartment under the bed." Shade walked up behind Waya as he opened the box. No fishing tackle was inside, but instead there were several 9mm clips of silver bullets, a small .22 caliber revolver presumably also loaded with silver, several hand grenades shaped like small cylinders, and what appeared to be a few containers of rock salt.

"I think you know about the silver, but these are incendiary grenades. Other than silver, fire is the best way to kill these things. If silver won't kill it, fire probably will, and vice versa, so as long as you have this tackle box you should be okay" Waya said before closing it back and returning it to its place under the boat seat. "The salt is for, well, ghosts I guess you'd call them. You'll know 'em if you see 'em, but they are rare and I don't think you'll be seeing any for a while. If you do, just toss some salt at 'em, should scatter 'em right quick. I already know you are familiar with the other weapons we have here, so I don't have to show you how to use the guns or explosives. Hell, I'm sure you're better with it all than I am anyway," Waya said as he stepped over to the steering platform and took yet another key from his key ring and started the boat, letting the engine idle.

"Untie us, would you?" he asked Shade, who hurriedly untied the boat so they could get started.

Waya started the engine and began to motor deeper into the swamp. "I guess I should explain a little more about these monsters and what it takes to kill them. If you see a big ass gator or snake or something, don't waste silver on it, just shoot the hell out of it with regular bullets or blow it up or something. Those things die like anything else. It just takes a lot to kill them. If it's something spooky, a werewolf or a damned vampire, silver for sure. And you don't have to shoot it a ton of times either. Silver is poison to them, one good shot and it usually drops them in a few seconds. You may want to pop 'em a few times to be sure, but once you deal with a few of 'em you'll see what I mean."

Shade secretly hoped he never had to deal with one, much less a few. As they rode along through the swamp and made their way under the tree canopy, Shade felt relaxed as he admired the beautiful scenery of the swamp. He'd always loved nature, but lately hadn't been able to appreciate it much. It felt like every time he was in a swamp or a jungle he was there to kill someone, and taking a moment to bond with nature just didn't fit into his time table. He saw the water break as fish jumped and saw some squirrels jumping through the trees. He was keeping his eye out for bloodthirsty beasts but at the moment it was very calm and serene. Shade found it hard to believe he was in such a scenic place and discussing things such as vampires and werewolves. The whole thing seemed absurd, but after what he'd seen and heard today he found it anything but.

"So what about those other things? The stuff that silver or fire won't work on? What are they and how do I deal with it?" Shade asked.

Waya shrugged, "Thankfully you won't see much of that. I'll show you how to get into our secret database on the computer. It's got information on any known monster and how to kill it. If it's not in there, we don't know how to kill it anyway. Oh, I will say this though. If you see any ghosts, we have some shotgun shells filled with salt; it's about the only thing that can take care of them. You can sometimes throw salt at them but that's not nearly as effective. The ghosts are bad, but rare. I've only seen one in all the time I've been here, so let's hope you never do. I mention them again because...well, if you ever see one, you'll know why."

Shade shook his head again, something he'd been doing a lot of today. Ghosts. On top of everything else the damn swamp was really haunted. Ain't that some shit? "Ghosts? Just what I needed to hear. You know after all the shit you've told me today, I have a feeling I may not ever sleep again."

"Eh, you'll get used to it. Somewhat at least," Waya said, realizing once he saw the swamp he never did get to sleep as soundly as he had before he knew it existed.

"Yeah I'll take your word for it," Shade said, the swamp growing darker and more ominous the deeper they went into it. "Damn, this place just feels wrong."

"Yeah, something's off in here for sure. I always think I know the place, then something scares the shit out of me and it's all messed up again. Weird-ass place."

Shade had a thought, "By the way, those incendiary grenades, how do I keep from staring a forest fire? I mean, I don't care so much about burning this swamp, but I'd hate for it to spread."

Waya shook his head, "Don't worry about it, damn place won't burn. You could spray every tree with the flamethrower and it wouldn't spread. Over the years people have tried to burn it, no luck. Government even tried to drain it back in the forties, not sure how they even found the damn place, but most of the workers were killed and they couldn't do anything with the place anyway. This shit-hole is here to stay."

"Speaking of the government, why haven't they sealed this place off and sent in the lab coats? This seems like the kind of thing the government would be all over," Shade asked. Even though he was patriotic, Shade knew about the darker side of politics. All the stories about monsters being used for warfare weren't exactly fiction. He was sure the government would love to get their hands on some of the creatures in the swamp.

"They have tried. It seems as though anytime you try to take one of these monsters out of the swamp the bodies only last for a few days before they just disappear, They turn to mist or some shit, I never got the full story. They tried to get around that by setting up a lab right in the swamp back in the 70s. Every scientist died in brutal ways, so they stopped with it. They even sent a military strike force in back in the 80s. Every one of them was killed too. Basically the government just washed their hands of this place. They give us the funding we need and just ignore it," Waya answered as he guided the boat deeper into the swamp.

"You mean to tell me with all of the crap the politicians love to dabble in, they actually found this swamp so bad they leave it alone? I didn't think it was possible for a place to even be that much trouble. And if a full military strike team couldn't deal with this place, how does a game warden handle it?" Shade asked.

"They weren't prepared for it. Even for all their training and weapons, I don't think they knew what they were getting into. And also, I don't think the United States wants any other countries getting wind of this place. Now, even if they do, they assume it is bullshit. If our people made too much of a fuss over it, though, the damn *bad guys* may start to believe the hype and try to find the place. I say we let 'em. I can't think of a better idea than letting a bunch of terrorists loose in this place." Waya appeared to be concentrating on his driving as the waterway narrowed.

"How much of my job is just in the boat like this, and how often will I need to be walking around on the ground back here?" Shade asked.

"That's a judgment call. We have four wheelers and other vehicles for driving around back here in the sheds. There are roads that lead around here but you have to be careful. They kinda change from day to day," Waya said, his tone of voice indicating he had no idea how that happened.

Shade shook his head. "Man, this place is really fucked up, isn't it?"

"Yeah, that's putting it mildly. And listen, another thing. From time to time you may find—things out here.. It's up to you whether you investigate it or just leave it alone, but I don't think I have to tell you that whatever you decide, *be careful.* If it's out here, it's bad."

"What do you mean by *things*? You've told me all about the *things* and even showed me pictures of the *things.*"

"I don't mean living things. I mean stuff like buildings, boats, things like that. I have seen cabins out here that were there one day and gone the next. Boats sometimes float up. I have even heard of a few ships that were found out here. One guy swears he saw a whole town. Just be careful, it may be best to avoid all of it, it usually just goes away on its own. Like I said, it's your call—you're the game warden now. And I hate to mention this part, but you have to know. Sometimes there's, well, *people* out here too. And they are hardly ever good people. It's hard to explain but be careful of anyone you meet in the swamp that you don't have any prior information on."

Shade was quizzical. "What do you mean exactly? What people?"

"Bad people. Just be careful," Waya said, not wanting to discuss the topic any longer.

"You know, in all the excitement I forgot to ask. What kinda salary and benefits are we talking about here? Do I get hazard pay or what?"

"You get paid like any other game warden in the state of Georgia. Same benefits. But, at the end of the year, let's just say your Christmas bonus will be a bit more than most."

"How much more? That's a pretty important bonus to me."

"It's right at a hundred grand. You make about fifty a year. It's good pay for a game warden, but for this place? Is there really any amount of money that would make it worth it?"

"I have never done a job for the money. I guess it's just about having something to do that will test my limits."

"This place will damn sure test your limits."

"Yeah, I have a feeling it will." The two rode along in silence for a few minutes as Shade wondered just what the hell he had gotten himself into.

THREE

Prohibition Era

Clem floored the old pickup and turned the sharp corner, almost slinging Jeb out of the cab as the truck went to two wheels for a split-second.

"Damn it Clem, if you want to kill me just take your damn pistol and shoot me in the damn head!" Jeb said, hanging on to the doorframe with one hand and his shotgun with the other.

The truck had no doors on it. They used this truck to run moonshine and sometimes needed to hop in and out in a hurry. The few seconds it took to open and close a door could be the difference between getting away clean and going to jail. It also made riding in the truck dangerous, especially when they were being pursued by local law enforcement as they were now. There were two police cars hot on their heels as they flew through the back roads, not sure where they were heading at this point but just trying to get away.

"Do you have any idea where you're going, you stupid sumbitch?" Jeb asked as Clem took another corner, once again almost dumping him from the vehicle.

"I'm just trying to get away from those bastards. Once we get away we can figure out where we are!" Clem said as he floored the truck again, the engine roaring.

"Try not to kill us at least! And we got six fifty-five-gallon drums of shine in the back, don't lose it! Eb will kill us!" Jeb said, referring to the boss of the operation.

"Eb can go to Hell. If it comes down to me going to jail or me losing the liquor, I will burn that shit up!" Clem said, something he'd never say in front of Eb.

"Hey what's that? That a road? Turn, Clem, turn!" Jeb said, spying a hidden turn-off that was barely visible from the roadway just at the edge of the truck's headlights.

Clem did one of his famous turns and sent the truck on two wheels, but made it. They found themselves on a dark, bumpy dirt road and Clem sped up, the truck bumping around and tossing them both around now. Jeb glanced back and saw both police cars speed past the road, obviously missing it. He bounced and felt his head hit the roof, causing him to see stars momentarily.

"Dammit, Clem slow down! They didn't follow us. You can at least slow down a little!" Jeb said, rubbing his sore head with his free hand.

Clem saw nothing but darkness behind them. He wasn't sure how they had missed the road, they had to have seen them turn off, but he was happy to have a moment to catch his breath.

The police report would say the truck had evaded pursuit. None of the police officers involved in the chase would be able to explain it. One second the vehicle had been right in front of them, and the next second it was gone. Both cars had driven up and down the stretch of road several times, both that night and the next day, and neither of them saw any trace of the truck or anywhere the truck could have been driven. It was like it had disappeared.

Clem and Jeb drove along the dirt road, the truck bumping as the road was in terrible shape. The road was very dark and narrow, the woods encroaching on it and barely allowing room for one lane of traffic.

"You have any idea where the hell we are?" Clem asked as he drove, waiting to see some type of landmark or sign of civilization.

"Nah, I never noticed this road before. But hell, I was lost before we even found it, so don't ask me," Jeb said, tightening his grip on the shotgun without realizing it.

The pair drove along in silence for another mile, the road unchanging. "Should I turn around? Maybe try to back us out of here?" Clem asked, getting nervous.

Jeb shook his head, "Nah, you can't turn us around here and it's too far to back up. It has to come out somewhere, let's just ride it out. You have plenty of gas?"

"Yeah I got half a tank, we're good for gas," Clem said. He was getting creeped out for some reason. Something about the road just felt *wrong*.

Suddenly the woods began to rustle, like a huge wind was tearing its way through. Before either man could speak, a growl rang out and turned into a scream and *something* crashed from the woods on the passenger side and smashed right into the side of the truck, rocking it.

"Holy shit, what the hell was that?" Jeb asked as the truck slid on the dirt road. Clem didn't want to find out and hit the gas, the truck spinning the dirt but getting traction as it took off down the dirt road.

Clem shifted in his seat as something huge and hairy grunted and rammed into the back of it, slamming both men forward. The truck turned to the side and both men panicked as it turned completely sideways, but Clem had done enough running from the law for his driving skills to be well-honed, and he managed to once again right the truck and send it speeding down the road.

"Dammit, Clem, what is that?" Jeb asked as Clem squinted in the rear view mirror trying to see just what was chasing them.

"I can't tell, it's just out of range of the tail lights, but the thing's fucking huge!" Clem said, his eyes wide.

The truck was jolted again as it was hit from behind, even though by now it was traveling along at fifty miles an hour down the bumpy road.

"How the hell is it still hitting us?" Jeb asked, leaning back to try to get a look at it. He aimed the shotgun behind the truck from the open doorway, being careful they didn't get bounced out or hit a tree that was too close to the road. He aimed behind and fired widely, firing both barrels of buckshot at whatever was behind them. They were rewarded with a squeal and the pursuer gave up the chase.

Clem didn't slow down in the slightest as Jeb reloaded. "You know if I didn't know any better..." Jeb said as he slid the shells home.

"That looked like a damn boar hog," Clem said.

"Damn sure did. But that fucker was as big as the truck! No way was that a boar!"

"Could it have been a rhino maybe? I think they get to be that size."

"You know, it could have been. Sure looked like a boar hog though, I got a good look at it a few times."

"Yeah I got a really good look at it in the tail lights. And it did look like a hog."

"Whatever the hell it was I hope it's gone. I was about to--"

Several things happened at once. The road suddenly opened up, the woods that were choking the roadway disappearing as they reached some type of clearing. The light also got brighter, as the leaves that had been blocking the moonlight went away. And finally, the truck slammed to a stop, going into a large sinkhole of mud with a sucking sound as both men were slammed into the windshield hard. Clem hit the steering wheel with his chest, knocking the air from his lungs. Jeb was smashed into his own shotgun, the barrel catching him right on the nose and breaking it with a crunch as blood gushed from his nostrils. Both the men cracked the windshield with their foreheads as water and mud began to seep into the open cabin.

"Ah shit that hurt! Jeb are you alive?" Clem asked, rubbing his chest with one hand and his forehead with the other.

"Yep but I fink I broke my doddamn nobe!" Jeb said, blowing the blood from his nostrils to clear them and sending blood and mucus all over himself and the interior of the truck, but at least allowing him to now speak clearly.

"Ew you nasty bastard, stop that!" Clem said, feeling some of the blood hit him and realizing what Jeb had just done.

"Aw shit, now my eye's swelling shut. This is some bullshit right here." Jeb said as his eye began to shut. "What the hell happened anyway?"

"I think we ran into a pond of something. And I think we're sinking, we better get the hell out of here," Clem answered as water and mud began to pour into the cab and the truck began to sink.

Both men floundered out, finding themselves in thick mud as they struggled towards the back of the truck, trying to find firm ground.

"Damn that truck's going down fast, this shit is quicksand. We just lost that whole damn load, too!" Jeb said as he held his shotgun over his head and walked along, wading in the thick mud that threatened to drag him under at any time.

"Oh shit, Eb is going to kill us!" Clem said as he practically swam though the viscous mud, making his way to shore.

"You just said he could go to Hell, what are you worried about?" Jeb replied, knowing Clem would never tell Eb that to his face.

Both men were lucky to make it out of the mud and lay on the bank panting as the truck sank deeper and deeper into the mire. They watched as the tail lights disappeared and the entire truck went under.

"Son of a bitch, it sucked the whole truck down!" Clem wasamazed at how fast it happened.

The two examined the area, the light of the moon the only illumination they had now as they tried to take in their surroundings. They were on the edge of a lake, or perhaps a swamp. Neither of them knew of any swamps in the immediate area.

"Do you have a flashlight on ya?" Jeb asked as he felt around in his pocket for his matches.

"Nah, I had one in the truck, but it's long gone now," Clem also searched his pockets but found his matches to be wet and ruined.

Jeb had put his matches in his breast pocket so was a little luckier. "Hot damn, I think my matches are dry!"

Both men then heard a hissing sound, as well as the squelch of something moving in the mud.

"What the hell is that sound? The truck hissing?" Jeb asked as he tried to get a match lit.

"I don't know, light the damn matches though, this dark is getting to me."

They squinted through the moonlight, but the dark mud and water of the swamp didn't betray any movement they could see. Then the hissing sound drew nearer.

"Dammit Jeb, light the damn matches!" Clem said as the sound neared him .

"All right, I got it, I got it!" Jeb said, able to strike a match.

The weak fire of the match served to light up a small area

of the swamp, but what it did light up appeared to be the triangular head of the biggest snake either man had ever seen. Even in the dim lighting, it appeared the snake was a Cottonmouth Moccasin, but its head was as wide as a man's body. Even the biggest constrictors of the Amazon River never reached the gigantic proportions of the serpent only inches away from Clem.

"Holy Shit, Jeb! Shoot it! SHOOT IT!" Clem yelled as he drew his pistol from his pocket, also wet and covered with mud.

Whether or not the pistol would have even fired would remain an unanswered question. Before Clem could even bring it up to fire, the giant snake struck, piercing Clem's torso with huge fangs that seemed to be over a foot long, and totally running his body through. Venom poured from the fangs and ran down Clem's back and legs, the fangs so long the venom was being injected outside of his body.

"Oh God Jeb, it hurts! It hurts so bad!" Clem screamed as the snake began to shake him back and forth in its jaws, coiling its long body around him and squeezing.

Jeb stood watching, frozen in place at the scene just a few feet away from him. As the match burned down to his fingers, he cursed and brought the shotgun up, but as the snake coiled around Clem, its huge body slammed into Jeb, knocking him to the ground. Jeb managed to hold onto the shotgun and from his back he raised the gun and fired both shots at the snake. He couldn't tell in the dim moonlight but he heard the snake hiss loudly so he assumed he had hit it. The snake ignored him, however, and was concentrating on Clem, who had gone silent.

Jeb struggled to his feet and ran, deciding there was nothing he could do for Clem and thinking once the snake finished eating it may come after him. He had a few shotgun shells in his coverall pockets which went forgotten as he ran screaming into the woods, not paying attention which direction he was running, just trying to get away from the nightmarish creature.

Jeb ran through thick woods, his feet sloshing in stagnant water ankle deep. He was still covered in mud from crawling out of the wreck as he searched for something, *anything* to help him survive this night.

In the distance he saw a dim light, so ran towards it

hoping to find help. The woods began to thin out, and Jeb saw a cabin in the distance. As he got closer he saw it was indeed a cabin, right on the bayou with a canoe on the bank nearby. The bayou was thankfully on the opposite side of the cabin from Jeb. Even in this state of panic, he wasn't going into any water after what he had just witnessed.

Jeb ran up to the cabin, a wooden shack with a tin roof that could have been over a hundred years old. It had a chimney and even in the dark night Jeb could see smoke, so hopefully someone was home.

Jeb walked up to the porch and laid the shotgun down, not wanting to frighten whoever was inside as at this point Jeb saw them as his only salvation. The cabin had no windows, so Jeb couldn't peek inside. He walked up to the door and knocked, trying to regain his composure. He realized between crawling through the mud and running through the woods, along with his bloodied nose, he'd be a fright to whoever answered, so the least he could do was calm down.

No one answered, so Jeb knocked again. This time he heard footsteps as someone walked around inside.

"Hello? Listen, I'm sorry, my friend and I wrecked our truck out here and I'm lost. Could I get some directions from you and maybe wait inside until the sun comes up? My name's Jeb and I live right outside of Savannah, I don't mean no harm, I just need some help," Jeb said, talking to the door and listening for movement.

The door opened suddenly, revealing a tall man dressed in overalls. "Oh thank you so much Sir, I—" Jeb never finished his sentence as an ax smashed right into his forehead, cleaving his skull in two and killing him instantly. Just before he died, Clem had a second to notice something was *wrong* with this man. He was mostly bald but did have strands of long, stringy hair growing haphazardly from his scalp. His teeth jutted from his mouth, and his lips were huge, like they were covered in bee stings. His eyes were different colors and were both crossed. He was a big man, and thick, and appeared very strong, so maybe nothing was wrong with him physically other than his appearance. The word *inbred* was what immediately came to mind when seeing him.

Jeb's body fell to the porch and the man put his foot on

his chest and wrenched the ax free. He searched outside the shack to see if the man had any friends with him, but decided he was alone. He grabbed Jeb by the legs and dragged his body into the shack, closing the door.

FOUR

The rest of the job interview had been uneventful, and Waya had taken the boat back to the office and let Shade go back home. Shade wasn't sure how to react to the initial swamp visit. On one hand, he was glad to get out of the swamp without having to fight a vampire or giant crocodile, but on the other hand, he would like to have seen *something* to validate what he had been told. The whole thing was just too weird. He still had a feeling Waya was just screwing with him, but the job itself seemed legit so he was going to play it out and see where things went. Shade was an only child, and he called his mother and father once he got home and told them of his new job. The two of them had retired to Miami, so he tried to give them a call at least once a week. He decided not to mention any of the "special game" his job might involve.

Shade showered again and as he lay in bed that night, he wondered if he would dream of monsters. He thought that may be a welcome change after dreaming of his friends dying every night for so long. He shut his eyes and fell asleep, and dreamt of nothing.

The next morning Shade showered and climbed in his SUV to make the trip to work. As he rode along, he wondered if he'd even be able to find the swamp again. That would be ironic, if after all that he'd find himself shut off from the place like everyone else. But he went right back to the road, and drove to the office without any further incident. Waya had told him to pack an overnight bag, as he wanted him to spend the night in the station for some immediate on-the-job training. Shade felt that was a bit much, spending the night in a haunted swamp on his first night, but he thought he should listen to Waya. Something about the old Indian made Shade feel as though he could be a good person to know.

    Shade pulled into his parking space beside Waya's pickup and climbed out, Waya waiting for him on the dock. Shade grabbed his small duffel bag and waved. He walked up to the office and pointed to his bag, indicating he was going to leave it inside. Waya nodded and began to walk towards him. Shade walked inside and put his bag on the bed in the apartment as Waya walked into the office after him.

    "How many nightmares did you have last night?" Waya said as way of a greeting.

    "I had none, or at least none I remember. Nightmares have become something I've had to get used to."

    Waya nodded. "Yes, I would reckon so. Oh, these are for you." Waya walked over and picked up a stack of clothing from the desk, handing the uniforms to Shade. He also handed him a pair of boots.

    "Already? Now that was fast," Shade said as he took them.

    "You're a pretty common size and we keep some in stock, so you're good to go. Why don't you go get changed while I work on some paperwork," Waya said, taking a seat behind the desk and starting to type on the computer.

    Shade went into the apartment and changed in a hurry, pleasantly surprised to find everything fit perfectly. Waya had let him take the firearm and gun belt home, so Shade removed them from his bag and put them on. He stepped in front of the mirror and found the new look appealed to him. He was now an official game warden, and looked the part. Only one thing was missing.

    Shade stepped out of the apartment and walked towards Waya. "Hey Waya, how about my—", he said, stopping as Waya held up his badge before he could even finish his sentence. Shade smiled and took it, affixing it to his shirt.

    "Here, take this one too," Waya said as he slid a wallet over to Shade. Once Shade had his badge firmly on his chest he picked up the wallet, flipping it open to a second badge inside.

    "What's the deal, why do I need 2 badges?" he asked as he put the wallet in his back pocket.

    "Shade, the badges are, let's just say, very important. They are your totem," Waya explained.

Shade was confused. "I don't understand."

Waya continued, "As we've said, the swamp does some weird things. It's huge and it's always changing. The badges act as guides. As long as you have a badge on you, you should always be able to find your way out. I used the meager Native American magic I possess to charm them for you. They may also protect you, so be sure to have one on you at all times."

"If I lose them, am I dead meat then?" Shade asked, already thinking of how easy it would be to find himself without a badge.

"No, it may not matter at all. We've had several game wardens lose their badges and they were fine until I got them another. We've also had some lose their badges and they were never seen again, just their badges were found. It just depends, but try your best to hold onto them. If I go over some of this stuff twice, I apologize, but I need to stress its importance."

Shade nodded, "I understand, and will do."

Waya typed a few minutes longer on the computer as Shade admired the swamp from the window. While it wasn't the most hospitable place, it really didn't appear that sinister. Waya finished and stood up, stretching his arms over his head.

"So what's on the agenda today, Chief?" Shade asked.

"I am going to handle some paperwork over in the Savannah office, and you are going to stay here and patrol the swamp a bit." Waya said as he stepped towards the door.

"Wait, what do you mean? I'm on my own already?" Shade asked surprised.

"Yeah, I do have another area to work. This swamp is basically part of the Savannah jurisdiction. We have to do it that way, otherwise we couldn't even get your mail to you—the mailman isn't even able to find the place. We just run everything through the Savannah office and this is the dirty little secret. Most of my time is spent out on the islands doing boring game warden stuff. You'll be handling this place on your own. If you need me, just give me a call." Waya said as he opened the door to leave.

"Hang on, just give you a call? Why do I have a feeling this place doesn't have the best cell phone reception?" Shade asked.

"There are radios in the storeroom, oh—and all the keys

are on the key ring in the upper right hand desk drawer, it's all you need. Just use the radio, I did a little mojo on 'em; you should be able to get me. I do have to get going though. Since you'll be staying the night, I'll drop back by once my shift ends to see how you did. Good luck!" Waya said and left before Shade could say anything else.

Shade stood in the office as he heard Waya drive away. The absurdity of the situation once again washed over him. Charmed badges? Magic radios? It was all strange.

Shade walked into the armory, opening all of the cabinets as he contemplated what he should bring with him. This was his first time out there solo, and he was planning on going out loaded for bear. Or loaded for whatever the hell else he may find.

He decided to take the M16 with the M203 grenade launcher mounted underneath it. He knew it was overkill, but damned if he was going to get killed on his first day. He grabbed an extra clip and a few grenades. Then he grabbed one clip of silver bullets for the M16 just in case. Waya had told him he would only need silver bullets for the machine guns in rare cases, but better safe than sorry.

Shade grabbed a radio and some binoculars before heading to the boat. He knew the boat had its own radio, but he might have to leave the boat and didn't want to be without a way to communicate. He opened the fridge, seeing Waya had left some sandwiches and water in a brown bag along with a note that said *You're Welcome, White Boy.* Shade smiled and went outside, going to the boat and dropping his items off. He put the food in the cooler and went back to his truck, getting his mirrored sunglasses and putting them on along with his State Trooper-style game warden hat. He felt pretty cool as he walked back into the office to retrieve his keys. He locked the place up before going to the boat and starting it up. He wanted to check out the sheds, but decided he could do that later.

As Shade drove the boat off into the swamp he was torn between feeling elated at the serenity of the area and being nervous at the potential danger. The day was very nice, slightly overcast with low humidity. Even the bugs weren't biting/.

The boat was equipped with a GPS, which was working fine at the moment. Shade knew he couldn't count on it, however, and also used the compass as a guide and made note of everything visually. He had a feeling he might need to find his way back without using any equipment at all.

He rode deep into the swamp, trying to get accustomed to all of the different areas. Sometimes he would be riding on huge bodies of water, like a lake or river, but then he would find himself on small creeks. A few times he had to back the boat out and try a different route, as the waterway had dried up. There were also acres and acres of somewhat dry land in the area, so not every inch of the swamp was wetlands after all. It was like no swamp he had ever seen, but that was not unexpected.

He jumped at every splash he heard, but so far had seen nothing to indicate the splashes had been anything other than fish. The birds were singing loudly and he had spotted several cranes and other species, but once again nothing out of the ordinary. A few times he had been startled by a rustling in the bushes, but had seen only squirrels. He even surprised two deer —a doe and its fawn—when he came around a bend in the swamp. The two were skittish and ran off. Shade wondered how things as harmless as deer and squirrels could possibly survive in a swamp filled with giant alligators and snakes. He didn't know Waya well, but something about him inspired trust. As crazy as it seemed, Shade did think the pictures in the photo album had been legitimate, but he still wondered about this place. What would bring such horror to a swamp in rural Georgia?

Shade spent most of the day just riding around in the boat, eating his sandwiches and sipping his water. He was amazed at the swamp's size. He never came close to reaching any of its boundaries before he decided he'd better head back. He didn't want to be caught in this swamp anywhere near dark, and intended to be back at the office before the sun had even begun to set.

The ride back was also uneventful, and Shade wasn't sure if he was disappointed or relieved to have had such a quiet day. He decided on relieved. He had a desire to see something that would solidify his belief that the swamp was "haunted," but he also knew if he ever did see something like that he would surely regret it. He shrugged and docked the boat, unloading all of the items he had brought, including the binoculars which he had never used.

As he walked back to the office, he noticed Waya's truck

was already there. The door was unlocked so he walked in to find Waya back at the desk and once again working on the computer.

"Hey, have you been here long? You should have radioed, I'd have come back sooner," Shade said as he laid some of his items on the desk. He took the machine gun, grenades and clip and headed for the armory.

Waya watched and saw what he was carrying. "I just got back, so no worries. But I have to ask, what the hell did you see that made you need that kinda firepower?" Waya's eyes widened as he saw the weaponry.

Shade laughed, "Nothing at all, I just figured better safe than sorry," he said as he put the guns and ammo back in place.

Waya called out from the office, "Damn, son, maybe I gave you the key to the weapons locker a little too soon!" he said with a chuckle.

Shade walked back into the office, smiling, "Nah, I was just being careful. The most dangerous things I saw out there today were a few deer and some squirrels. I didn't even see a single alligator, or even a snake. The only things out there that bite were the mosquitoes, and I met a few of them." Shade said, scratching a few bites for emphasis.

"Like I was saying, today was a typical day. You'll have hundreds of slow days, and hopefully only a handful where you deal with something shitty. Who knows, maybe you'll never see any of the bad stuff!" Waya said, although it sounded hollow.

"Now, what do I need to do as far as paperwork and reports go?" Shade asked, looking at Waya expectantly.

"Don't worry about it for tonight. As a matter of fact, what I want you to spend the night doing is going through the handbook and flipping through these notebooks. Most of the stuff you do around here is just filling in blanks on the computer and it's all pretty routine. There is a, uh, *special* form you might to fill out if it comes to that, but it's all in the notebooks here." Waya waved his hand at the bookshelf behind the desk.

"So just read the handbook and notebooks and it's pretty much self-explanatory?" Shade said, knowing a little about governmental regulations.

"Yep, it's all there. And don't worry about memorizing all of this shit either. If you need to look it up, just look it up. There's a handbook in the glove compartment of the boat and the truck, too."

Shade nodded and realized he hadn't checked boat's glove compartment all day, and hadn't even been in the SUV yet.

Waya took a flash drive from the computer and then stood and headed towards the door. "Damn, I almost forgot a few very important things. As you can guess, we don't have Internet service out here in the haunted swamp. Every day I come out with a flash drive and update this computer with current information. You obviously don't have the entire database here, but I try to keep it up-to-date with the most important stuff. Anything you enter, I will also put on a flash drive and add it to the database from my other office computer. Not *anything* you enter, but any of the normal game warden paperwork."

Shade nodded, realizing he hadn't even thought of the computer not being connected to the Internet before now.

Waya continued, "Another thing, you might be wondering how we get power out here. There's a small shed directly behind the office, it contains the generator. We have our own gas tank here, and I drive a tanker in every other week and fill the tank up myself. The generator is tied directly into the tank. You'll need to go out and check the generator every few days just to be sure it's working. We soundproofed the shed otherwise we couldn't hear ourselves think. That's not why we soundproofed it though. The noise was attracting...*things.* The generator will be fine tonight, so no worries, but I should have mentioned that to you earlier."

Waya paused as if thinking of any other information Shade may need to know. He then nodded, satisfied. "Now, I need to get out of here before dark. For obvious reasons, it's best not to be on this road once the sun goes down. I would say you just kick back in the cabin and read tonight. There's some pizza in the fridge that I brought you for dinner, and some beer, too. You aren't supposed to drink on the job, but a few beers shouldn't hurt you, especially since you're only *technically* on duty," Waya said with a wink. "The TV here doesn't work - no reception - and the radio only plays when it wants to, but there are some CDs back there if you want to listen to some music."

Shade shook his head. "I think I'll just read tonight and turn in early. The sooner it gets daylight around here, the better, I think, so I'd rather spend the dark sleeping."

Waya made pistol shapes with his thumbs and forefingers

and pointed them both at Shade, firing them. "Good idea! Well, you have a good night. If you, uh, hear anything, it's up to you what to do about it. If you want to ignore it, that's fine, I don't think the world will end on your first night here. If you feel adventurous and want to check it out, *be careful.* And don't hesitate to call or radio me if you need to, if nothing else I may be able to give you some advice."

Shade nodded, "Thanks, Waya, seriously."

Waya nodded back and left. Shade watched through the glass door as Waya's truck disappeared down the long dirt road. Shade figured he had maybe an hour of daylight left, so he went outside to make sure everything was secure before bedding down for the night. He checked the boat and found it secured, and made sure the sheds were locked. He still wanted to check them out, but there was time for that later. He made sure the truck was locked before heading inside and locking the office. There were two entrances to the office: the front door and a back door that opened from the apartment. He made sure both doors were firmly locked before he grabbed the handbook and started to flip through it.

He got a slice of pizza out and began to eat it cold, devouring the entire slice before he even opened a beer. He took a few sips of beer and read through the handbook, then ate a second slice of pizza before finishing the beer. By this point it was pitch black outside, but there were a few large lights on poles in the parking lot and over the dock, which kept the entire area very well lit. He fed the fish in the aquarium and left one light on over the office desk before undressing and laying on the bed on top of the covers. He decided he would shower in the morning.

He managed to read most of the handbook before putting it on the nightstand and turning the lamp off. He was asleep in seconds.

Shade woke up to the sounds of laughing children. He blinked his eyes a few times and squinted at the alarm clock. It was after three am. Was he dreaming? He listened for a few seconds and heard nothing, so he promptly went back to sleep.

Laughter woke him again a few minutes later. He sat up

in bed and rubbed his eyes, trying to figure out what was going on. Did he leave a radio on? Did the TV start working? He heard a high-pitched giggle and then the good-natured screams of children playing together. *What the hell is going on?*

Shade stood and walked to the window, which faced the dock house with a good view of the bay. He shook his head and rubbed his eyes again. Just at the edge of the light projected from the outside lamp, Shade could swear he saw a playground in the swamp with several children playing. He squinted as his heart began to beat faster and his breath shortened. This was impossible. The area the playground now occupied was supposed to be water, and had been water a few hours earlier. Shade watched for a few minutes. The moon was dim tonight and the playground was mostly out of range of the light, so he didn't have a good view of exactly what was happening; he could only see vague outlines.

As he watched, a small girl of maybe seven years old chased a ball to the edge of the playground, giggling as she caught it. Several more children appeared, chasing her as she ran back into the dark of the playground. Shade debated whether to go outside and figure this out, or just to go back to bed and hope it was gone in the morning. His curiosity got the better of him and he got dressed, slipping into his uniform and being sure he had both badges and his gun belt. He started to walk outside and stopped, going back and checking under the bed instead. There was a toolbox under the bed which he pulled out and sat at the foot of the bed before opening. It contained the same bullets, grenades and salt containers as the one in the boat. He shut it and brought it along just in case.

Shade walked over to the dock, trying to get a better view of the playground. Sure enough, an island had popped up right at the edge of the small lake, and there was a playground occupying the island. He walked along the dock and was able to see the monkey bars, a slide, a see-saw, a merry-go-round, and swings. He counted eight children, all of them in various stages of play. Once again, their giggling echoed in the night, sending chills down his spine.

Something was sinister about an empty playground at night. The fact this one had giggling children playing on it at three in the morning, just made it worse. His first night in, and the swamp was already messing with him. He just stood and watched a while, trying to decide his next course of action.

The girl he had first seen had long blonde hair and was wearing a white dress. She was dressed in an antique style, wearing something a little girl would have worn in the 1800s. One of the boys ran closer and Shade saw he was definitely dressed as a child from the past. He had on a velvet suit with knee-length pants, and he had a lace blouse on with a frilly white collar. The boy even appeared to be wearing stockings and black patent shoes. Another child on the swing was wearing red overalls and tennis shoes. Shade supposed that could be a modern style of dress but looked like something from the 1950s. Two black children were on the seesaw, and although Shade couldn't swear to it, they were dressed as slave children would have been in the days before the Civil War.

He swallowed hard as he watched the children playing and laughing. It was like children from different time periods had all been thrown together on the same playground. He stood in place watching the children play until the tool box began to get heavy in his hand. So far none of the children had paid him any mind and were content to play with one another.

Shade was still debating his next course of action with the blonde girl spotted him. She laughed and tugged on the shirt of the boy next to her, the one with the knee length trousers. They all waved the other children over, and all of them stood near the edge of the playground laughing at Shade.

Shade smiled and waved at them as they smiled and waved back. They began to wave him over, motioning him to join them.

"Come play with us!" they chanted.

Shade smiled and walked towards the end of the dock. The island was only a few feet away from the dock at the far end, and Shade could easily hop onto the island from there. He smiled as he walked over. *All they wanted was to play. Why had he been frightened?* He moved as in a dream, still carrying the toolbox as he hopped onto the island.

The children giggled and ran over to him, all of them surrounding him and hopping up and down as they sang in unison.

"Play with us! Play with us! Play with us!" Their voices

droned into Shades head and he staggered onto the playground as if drunk. He walked over and sat on the swing, putting his toolbox on the ground beside him as the children began to push him, swinging him high with each push. He grinned, lost in a fever as he watched the world swirl before him.

Something's wrong, he thought as the giggles of the children blanketed his brain. *This isn't right. THIS ISN'T RIGHT!*

The boy in the velvet outfit was now swinging right beside Shade and he watched the child giggle at him as they both swung in unison. The moon was a little brighter now, and as the child swung into the moonlight, Shade saw him become transparent. He could see right through the boy. Shade watched the other children surrounding him and noticed they were also transparent. They were ghostly white and translucent as their bodies flowed like mist. He turned back towards the velvet boy and saw his face morph into a skull as his eyes glowed red and his teeth became fangs. Shade screamed and put his feet down, trying to stop himself from swinging.

Everything was in slow motion as Shade's feet dragged along the dirt and the children all around him abruptly became monstrous apparitions. They all appeared to be made of mist now and their faces shifted from children's faces to skulls depending on how the moonlight struck them. Their eyes were all glowing red and they appeared to have fangs and also claws now. Shade felt them ripping and tearing at him, the formless shapes solid as his shoulder was bitten deep by the blonde girl and the other children bit and clawed at him.

Shade finally managed to stop himself, falling face first onto the dirt as the ghosts swarmed him, ripping and tearing his flesh as they gnawed and scratched. Twin fangs sank deep into his calf as claws ripped across his scalp, bloodying it. He drew his gun and began to fire into the mass, the bullets passing harmlessly through the specters as he emptied his clip into the night.

He was unable to move under the weight of the ghosts as they piled on top of him. He fought back, swinging and kicking, but found himself unable to connect with them even though they had no problem touching him. It was like fighting air as he found himself being torn to pieces by the phantoms. The giggling echoed in his skull, making him dizzy as they laughed while they mauled him.

Shade wasn't going down without a fight and kept kicking and swinging from the ground, his foot catching the toolbox and slamming it against the swing post. Almost immediately, one of the ghost children shrieked, a blood curdling scream unlike any sounds the ghosts had made so far. Shade watched as the ghost swiftly winked out. One second it was there, the next it had disappeared. By now, blood was pouring into Shade's eyes as the other ghosts stopped attacking for the moment, as if unsure themselves what was going on. Shade managed to squint through his crimson-tinted vision and see what had happened. When his foot had struck the toolbox, it had broken open and the contents had poured out onto the ground. One of the boxes of salt had come open and some of the salt had spilled against one of the ghosts.

Shade gritted his teeth and scrambled along the dirt towards the salt as the ghosts swarmed him again. Shade grabbed up a handful of salt, getting dirt along with it as he slung the handful of grit into the mass of evil children attacking him. He was rewarded with several more shrieks and a few more ghosts winked out of existence.

The few that were left attacked with renewed zeal, but by this time Shade had managed to grab the box of salt and was slinging it at the remaining haunts by the handful.

"Take that you little bastards!" he growled as the watched the expressions on their faces turn to horror as they went back to whatever Hell spawned them. He used the last of the box of salt on the two remaining ghosts and watched as they disappeared.

Shade panted as he lay bleeding in the playground, alone now, hoping he had managed to destroy the ghosts. He rubbed the blood out of his eyes and sobbed at the situation. He had never believed in ghosts, but now he had no choice. He had fought in the most dangerous parts of the worlds against the most dangerous men alive, but had nearly been killed by a bunch of children who had died long ago. It was too much to handle, but he was a Navy SEAL and he'd get through this the same way he got through everything else.

Shade sat up, trying to do a mental inventory on his wounds as he surveyed the playground. It was a real playground, just as it appeared. How the hell did it get here? It was ancient and rusting, possibly abandoned for decades.

Shade gathered up the contents of the toolbox and shut it, lying flat on the ground as he tried to catch his breath. He didn't think he was seriously wounded, but he needed to get inside and check himself over just in case.

As Shade lay down, closing his eyes to rest for just a second, he suddenly felt wet, moisture was seeping up from the ground. He lifted his head up. The playground was sinking, and fast. Shade managed to climb to his feet, grabbing the toolbox as he ran, his wounds burning but not stopping him as he stumbled towards the dock. The water was already ankle deep, and the last thing he wanted was find himself in the swamp after dark. He ran over to the edge of the island and tossed the toolbox up onto the dock as he jumped onto it himself, once again rolling over and lying flat as he watched the playground sink. It was a matter of seconds before it was totally submerged, a few bubbles rising from the water the only sign it had ever existed. *What the hell have I gotten myself into?* He asked himself, not for the first time, nor would it be the last. He stood up and walked back into the office, going right into the apartment and dropping the toolbox onto the floor, collapsing onto the bed and falling into a deep sleep.

FIVE

Shade woke up the next morning to find himself battered and bruised. He was face-down on the bed and he lay there for a few minutes, hoping that the night before had just been a horrible nightmare. He realized he was still wearing his uniform and that the events of the night before might have happened. He rolled over and sat on the edge of the bed, rubbing his face in his hands. He was still wearing his gun belt, so he drew his pistol and checked it for ammo. It was empty. The evidence was piling up against the nightmare theory. The alarm clock showed six-thirty. Shade hoped that was am and not pm. He was feeling so discombobulated it could have been either. He lifted his head and peered outside and saw the sun was just beginning to rise and a mist lay over everything outdoors. So it was six-thirty in the morning after all.

Shade stood and looked at the bed, then down at himself. There was no blood to be found on the sheets, or on his uniform. His uniform was also intact, other than being very wrinkled. When he tumbled into bed last night he was bleeding from a dozen wounds and his uniform had been torn and shredded. He walked into the bathroom and flipped the light on, examining himself in the mirror. He did have light scratches on his face and scalp, and the areas were tender, but nothing like they should have been. He pulled his shirt off and saw the same thing—mild wounds and scratches but nothing serious.

He shook his head and undressed, climbing into the shower and letting the cold water run over him. He had some medication at home the doctors had prescribed him, but after seeing how bad prescription medication had messed up some of his fellow soldiers, he had decided not to partake. If he had brought the pills along, however, he would have taken some now.

As the water washed over him, Shade tried to put together

exactly what had happened last night. He remembered the playground and the children. The children were some type of evil spirits, and had done something to him, like hypnotism. They had tried to kill him but he had managed to survive through mostly dumb luck. He also remembered the playground sinking back beneath the swamp. He had a feeling that no matter how hard he tried to find the rusted playground equipment under the black water of the swamp he would fail. It had gone somewhere other than just below the water, and wherever it had gone, he hoped it stayed.

He finished getting dressed and reloaded his firearm, then took the toolbox into the armory to replenish and rearrange the items. He was beginning to see that he would never go into the swamp again without one of the boxes, and also thought he should carry some of the big guns each time.

He made some coffee and went into the office, getting the manual back out and checking out the computer to see if he needed to do any start-of-day paperwork. He had yet to check the swamp to see if the playground had reappeared. He didn't even want to know until he had his first cup of coffee.

As he typed in some information on the keyboard, he heard Waya's truck pull up outside. He wasn't sure if he wanted to hug Waya or kill him, so decided he better just sit tight for now. Waya came in using his own key and saw Shade sitting at the computer.

"Hey, you made it! Not that I doubted you, but, you know, it's still good to see you decided to stick around," Waya said, smiling with relief. Shade could tell by Waya's reaction that he had thought there was a chance Shade would either have bolted by now or perhaps not even have survived.

"Yeah I'm here for now, but I'm still wondering about this job," Shade said, giving Waya a hard look.

Waya's face dropped and he knew something had happened. He examined Shade's face and head. "What happened, did you get caught up in some brambles or something?" Waya asked, realizing it sounded stupid but not wanting to consider the alternatives.

"Yeah, or something. A damn playground full of ghost kids tried to punch my damn ticket last night. Scariest shit I've ever been through in my life. Give me some terrorists to fight any day," Shade said, going back to punching keys.

"Ghost kids? Your first night here? Damn, this place is getting worse," Waya said as he took a seat in front of the desk and rubbed his chin, thinking. "Tell me more?"

Shade stopped with the computer entries for now and told Waya the complete story of the night before, as best he could remember it. Waya listened, nodding a few times, but never doubting what he was hearing or being surprised by any of it. Shade thought this was a bad sign. He had hoped a playground full of killer ghost children would be something new and not something that happened around here all of the time.

When Shade was finished Waya stared into space lost in thought. "So, what the hell, Waya? Is this kinda shit going to happen to me all the time here? I knew you said this place could be bad, but I didn't realize it would be like that 24/7."

"I'm not sure what to make of this. Like I told you yesterday, we do have ghosts here from time to time, but I've never heard of anything like that. I suppose maybe back in the old days something could have gone down, but not since we've been keeping track of things here. I think the place is getting worse, and that worries me," Waya said, once again staring into space, lost in thought. Something about the way Waya said the last sentence sent chills down Shade's spine.

"You know, I may not be the man for the job after all, Waya. I mean I've been through some heavy shit, but nothing *this* heavy. I may need to just walk away now before something makes the choice for me." Shade said standing up and walking over to the window now. As expected, there was no sign the playground had ever been there.

"I usually tell this part of the story gradually, but I guess I need to tell you more now. Have a seat, Shade, and let me tell you all I know of the swamp, and how it relates to you. Once you've heard me out, you can make your choice then."

"That sounds a lot like the speech you gave me yesterday."

"Please, I promise this is very important. Sit and let me tell you what I know." Waya implored, motioning Shade back to the chair behind the desk.

Shade instead walked around and took the seat right next to Waya. "Talk to me."

Waya began to speak. "This swamp, it goes back many generations in the Cherokee Nation. My grandfather's grandfather has told stories of this swamp. At one time, there was even a burial ground here, as most haunted places always seem to have. No one is sure exactly what this place is—we only know it is evil. Some think it's a gateway that leads straight to Hell, others think it's just a gateway to another dimension. No one is sure.

"Back in the ancient days, there was a great Cherokee medicine man. He was known as Bly, which means tall. He had been fighting the swamp and its' evils for many years, and he said the swamp was a greedy beast, and it was growing. He knew that if he didn't stop the swamp then, it would continue to grow until it covered the entire Earth. So he called upon the great spirits to help him. He gave his life to prevent the swamp from spreading its evil. The swamp has been contained ever since then."

"I thought you said you weren't sure how big the swamp was, that it could be huge?" Shade asked.

"Ah, that is the inside of the swamp. Back then, the swamp was growing outside. To explain it clearer, let's say the swamp is a gateway to another place. The deeper you to into the swamp, the further into the other place you go. Back in the day of Bly, the swamp was coming out of the gate, and covering *this* place instead. If Bly hadn't acted, all of Earth could have been part of that other place."

Shade nodded, "I think I know what you mean. Please go on."

Waya continued, "Bly did a great spell, which has been lost as time goes by. His death allowed him to stop the swamp from taking over, but didn't allow him to take back what the swamp had already claimed. The spell had another use as well. It allowed a guardian to be chosen, someone who could defend the world from the swamp and its horrors. Only one guardian can exist at a time."

"So you're saying I'm that guardian?"

Waya nodded, "You are indeed. You have been chosen."

"Chosen by whom? Bly? I don't understand that part, who

does the choosing, and why me?" Shade said, getting a little upset now.

"No one knows exactly who does the choosing, but ever since Bly sacrificed himself hundreds of years ago, a guardian has always been chosen. A game warden, if you will."

"But why would it choose a white man? And how do you keep coming in here? Are you doing the choosing? There are too many damn unanswered questions!"

"Please calm yourself, Shade. I am only able to do the things I do because my bloodline goes back years and years and I am a fully trained Cherokee shaman. My son was also in training, before this damned swamp took him from me. And as far as you being a white man, the spell is color blind. There have been black, white, Indian, Spanish and even a few Asian game wardens over the years."

"I get the feeling this job does have a high turnover rate. Now, out of all these guardians you just named, how many have voluntarily retired and how many were forcibly retired, if you know what I mean?"

"It is true the swamp has claimed the lives of many game wardens over the years, but there have been cases where a new guardian is chosen and the old one moves on. They retire on a game warden's pension and die of old age. It's happened several times."

"So what, a new guy just shows up and the old guy leaves? How does that work?"

"It's happened in several ways. There are some who simply can't handle the job, and they quit. Eventually a new guardian shows up, hopefully before too much havoc is wreaked by the swamp. You aren't a prisoner here, Shade, but you were chosen for a reason."

"What reason?"

"That is up for you to decide."

Shade stared at Waya for a few minutes as neither man spoke. Shade had to admit his life had been directionless since he got back to the States. Guarding the world from an insidious evil was definitely a direction.

Waya stood and walked to the desk, taking out the aged photo album. He flipped it open to the first page and pointed to the very first picture. "This guy, the one holding the gun standing by the giant crocodile. Do you recognize him?"

Shade squinted and tried to think. The man wasn't familiar to him, but Shade assumed he must be someone famous. "No, he's a little before my time, who is he?"

"Your great-great-grandfather." Waya said.

Shade's jaw dropped as he examined the man. He had no knowledge of his family going that far back, but he did admit even in the antique sepia photograph he could see a possible family resemblance. "Did you know that before I got here?"

Waya shook his head, "No, I did some research yesterday and found out. Most of the game wardens who work here have had relatives serve as game wardens before. I suppose it's something to do with the bloodlines. Your family has a good history here, Shade. They have saved the world from many evils over the years."

Shade stared at the picture and then began to flip through the album, "Do I have other relatives in some of these pictures?"

"I am sure you do, but I haven't had a chance to research them all yet. You do have roots here, Shade. I would be honored if you would stay."

Shade flipped through the pictures several times before closing the album and setting it down on the desk. He sighed. "If I already survived one of the worst things you've heard come out of this shit-hole, I guess I'm ahead of the game, right?"

Waya smiled, "Yes, you are definitely ahead of the game. Thank you, and welcome aboard."

SIX

The 1600s, Height of Piracy on the High Seas

"You'll never take me alive!" Captain Jervis Finnegan yelled at the British ship that was currently chasing him and his ship, the *King Anne*, across the Atlantic Ocean. He had named his ship as a direct insult to the King. "You'll all be in hell waiting for a long time before I arrive!"

Captain Finnegan, also known as Earless, had been prowling the ocean off Savannah's coast for months, raiding every merchant ship he could find heading for the River Street Port. The city had many who were friendly to pirates, and Earless —who many called Fearless Earless—had managed to stay one step ahead of the British Navy for a while now. His name was not just hyperbole as he had lost both ears when he had been captured and they attempted to hang him, but his fellow pirate had managed to free him just before he could be executed. However, in freeing him from the hangman's noose, both of his ears had been ripped off and he now had neither. His eardrums were still intact, however, and his hearing was fine.

Earless had finally been caught in an ambush when one of his men had turned on him after one too many beatings. The Navy had been waiting for Earless just off the coast of Savannah, and had captured two of his three ships, but the one Earless himself was aboard had managed to escape in the confusion, although it had a British Man-of-War in hot pursuit.

"You can chase me all you want you sons-of-bitches, but you'll never catch me!" Earless yelled back at the ship defiantly. The crew all knew there was no way anyone on the ship could hear the captain, and honestly the captain did too, but bravado went a long way among pirate crews, and the fiercer you were, the better.

The crew began to get a little nervous as it was becoming obvious the British ship was gradually gaining on them. They were doing all they could for speed and were concerned the captain might start throwing men overboard soon to lighten the load, but at this point even that would be futile. If something didn't change soon the only options would be surrender or fight. Piracy was still a hanging offense—something Earless knew all too well—so fighting would be the most likely option. But the British crew was filled with trained soldiers much better equipped than the pirates, not like the smaller and practically unarmed crews on the merchant vessels. The pirates all knew their time could be coming to an end soon.

The ship had been skirting the coast and staying in sight of land, hoping to find something, anything, that could help them escape. The ship was too large to run onto the beach, and they didn't have time to launch any smaller boats to escape by land. Things were getting desperate, and no one was sure what to do.

A mist began to appear, even though the day was very clear with white clouds and blue sky overhead. The crew wondered what was happening as the mist began to thicken.

"I'll be damned. If this mist gets much thicker we may be able to lose the bastards!" Earless shouted, seeing some hope in the situation.

The other crew members were quiet. Sailors, as a rule, are a superstitious lot, and this mist suddenly appearing from nowhere was as unnerving to them as the war ship behind them. They had heard tales of ships sailing into similar mists and never being seen again. Each of them pondered what would be worse—dying at the end of a rope or sailing forever on a ghost ship from Hell.

"Hey now, wot's that!" Earless said, pointing to a large channel that had come into view. "There! Right there, head us right in! Now, dammit, now!"

The crew obeyed and sailed right into the newly discovered channel, the mist so thick now the pursuing ship was totally lost from view. Records from the time period would say the ship had sailed into a bank of fog and disappeared, never to be seen again. The British ship had sailed through the area several times, the fog eventually dissipating. They had also combed the area several times for weeks, including a crude search of the area to see if perhaps the ship had been sunk. They never found any sign of the ship, and it faded into legend as one of the many nautical mysteries that were famous for the time period.

The *King Anne* sailed deep into the channel, the fog so thick the crew could barely see the land. The waterway wasn't very wide, and the ship barely fit. The crew was concerned the water might become too shallow at any time, but they continually checked the depth and had no issues.

"I've sailed this area a hundred times, and I've never seen this channel before," Earless said as he tried his best to squint through the fog, "Just where the hell have we ended up?"

The fog disappeared as fast as it had appeared, and the men found themselves in what appeared to be a small lake. It appeared they had sailed right into the middle of a swamp.

"Weigh anchor! And hurry before you run us aground, you sons of whores!" Earless shouted as the crew worked to bring the ship to a halt. They managed to stop the *King Anne* without incident and the crew tried to determine their location.

"I guess we lost those bastards after all! They missed the channel or were too chicken shit to follow us! Rejoice, lads, we've screwed the King again!" Earless said, getting a half-hearted yell from the crew. They were all too uneasy about the current happenings to celebrate.

"I suppose maybe we should stay here, but let's try to turn the ship around to face the channel so we can catch them if they do happen to grow the balls to follow us!" Earless shouted as the crew went to work again, trying to reposition the ship in the lake so it could bring its cannons to bear if any ships came down the channel.

"Cap'n, do ye think maybe land could be an issue? Could the navy have sent us down 'ere and have cannon ashore out of sight or somethin?" the first mate, known as Charley, asked.

"Nay, I don't think so. We are in the heart of a swamp. I don't think they could even get a cannon in if they tried," Earless answered as he surveyed the banks, noticing it was marsh and much too soft for ground troops.

As the ship turned, the men noted something unusual. The

channel they had just sailed down had shrunk. It was basically just a wide canal now, and there was no way a ship the size of the *King Anne* could have made it through.

"What the hell are you men doing? That's not the right channel! Sail us to the wide one!" Earless ordered, still not realizing the situation.

"Cap'n, I think that is the channel," Charley said, gulping.

The crew peered at the edge of the lagoon, trying to see if there was another way out and if perhaps they somehow had gotten turned around and missed the channel. Earless even got his spyglass out, but the narrow stream appeared to be the only waterway that entered the area.

"What the hell is going on? Did the tide come in or go out or something? What happened to the damned channel?" Earless asked as the entire crew edged closer to utter panic.

"Calm down ya bunch of scurvy dogs! Are ye men or are ye mice? Now calm down and let's think about this!" Earless ordered, his authority managing to calm the crew slightly, but he knew he would soon lose all control of these men if he couldn't think of a solution for this dilemma.

"Now listen, here's what we'll do. We'll take the long boat and check out the bank and see what we can find, maybe we can put ashore somewhere here and find our way to civilized people," Earless ordered.

"Now, Charley and I will take five crew members, you, you, and the three of you," Earless said as he picked three at random, the crew members basically being faceless and interchangeable to him. "The rest of you sit tight on the ship and try not to shit yer knickers."

The seven men loaded the muskets and pistols and climbed into the long boat. They all made sure they had their cutlasses. They didn't expect to meet any opposition, but better safe than sorry. The other crew members watched as the boat was lowered and the men began to paddle away towards shore. The crew wasn't sure which was better, being stuck on the big ship in the middle of nowhere, or being on the tiny boat in the middle of nowhere. The smaller boat was at least going somewhere, but the larger ship did feel safer overall.

As the skiff was rowed away, Earless called to the crew, "Don't worry, mates, we'll be fine!"

Suddenly a cry split the air, "Kraken! By God, it's a Kraken!" one of the crew members aboard the ship called, The crew on the ship flew into total panic, rushing to and fro with no rhyme or reason before they even saw the threat for themselves. The Kraken, or giant octopus, was a legend known by any who sailed the seas.

"What the hell are they going on about? There's no damned Kraken! Stop acting as if you should all be wearing skirts and calm down!" Earless demanded.

Huge tentacles erupted from all around the ship then, shooting up from the briny depths with an explosive force as they towered high above even the tallest mast of the ship. The men on board went into total panic and the men paddling the skiff began rowing faster, trying to get further away from the ship as the tentacles began to encircle it.

"My god, it is a Kraken..." Earless said, his jaw dropping as he watched the tentacles wrapping around the *King Anne*.

The tentacles encircled the entire ship and tightened, crushing the huge vessel like it was made of basalt wood as it splintered and went to pieces under its grip. Men were firing and hacking at the tentacles to no avail as it broke the ship up into kindling. Several of the men were crushed by the huge tentacles and a few others had the suction cups rip organs from their bodies as they were caught in just the wrong places at the wrong time. Several of the men leaped from the ship as the entire shattered craft was dragged under the water. The black liquid frothed and churned as the ship disappeared from view entirely, something that seemed impossible given the limited size of the lagoon. The speed with which the ship had been destroyed was also shocking—it had taken only seconds for the entire vessel to be sucked into the black depths.

A few crew members were trying to swim to safety, and the force of the undertow sucked several of them down, never to be seen again. The few that had survived the capsizing were swimming for the longboat, but before they could reach it, tentacles came up from below and dragged them under as well, their screams being cut short as the dark brine was sucked into their lungs.

The skiff was near shore now, and even before the bow hit land the men were scrambling out, stomping their way onto the muddy marsh grass to get away from the horror that had just killed all forty of their fellow crew members. Captain Earless was the last to exit the skiff, shuffling in a trance, the mud sucking at his boots as he made his way ashore. The men were running as best they could through the soft ground, afraid that at any moment the huge tentacles would pluck them from the very earth and drag them to their doom. Given the apparent size of the devilfish, such an act might be possible.

The men ran deeper into the swamp, now entering the tree-lined area as the ground got firmer. They didn't stop until they were out of the sight of the lagoon and trees were all around them. They collapsed to catch their breath as the horror of what they had witnessed began to numb them all.

Captain Earless sat and leaned his back against an oak tree, staring off into space as the screams of the men echoed in his ears. The screams of dying men were not new to Earless—he had sent scores of men to their deaths in his career—but he had never seen anything like that. For all the legends of the Kraken, he had always thought it a myth, and had never seen anything to convince him otherwise. Until today.

"Cap'n, what now?" Charley asked, the other men turning to Earless expectantly.

Earless scowled at each man before answering. "Now we just head through the swamp until we find some people or some dry land. We have to hit something eventually, and God knows we don't want to head back towards that damn devilfish."

The men nodded, happy to let someone else do the thinking for them, as their brains were not functioning properly at that moment. They all stood and followed Earless as he picked a random direction and began to walk through the swamp. Thankfully, each of the men had a canteen with them, and even though it was a small amount of water, it was better than nothing. They didn't plan on being lost for long.

The men walked through the swamp for hours, sometimes having to circle around to avoid bodies of water, as none of them wanted to risk it. Sometimes the swamp would get so soft it would be impassable, so they had to find a new route. After a few hours, they all knew they were hopelessly lost.

They had stopped to rest, no one speaking, as they all watched the sun begin to set. They were contemplating whether to keep walking or stop for the night. Even though a Kraken shouldn't be able to reach them here, the swamp still had plenty of snakes and alligators that could, as well as the mosquitoes and gnats that had been sucking them dry all day. The humidity was unbearable here, and their clothes were all soaked with perspiration.

Before anyone could speak, the men heard what sounded like a crowd of people walking nearby. They heard human voices too, although they couldn't make out any words, just grunts and groans.

"Eh now, I think I hear the sounds of civilization!" Earless said with a grin. The others all grinned along with him and, with renewed vigor, crashed through the woods in the direction of the sounds.

They soon emerged into a clearing, and sure enough, several people were standing around. It was quite a crowd, as what appeared to be about twenty men and women were in the clearing. The sun was going down and it was hard to make out the group clearly, but it appeared to be a group of slaves. They were all dressed in the fashion of slaves at the time, and they appeared to be African.

"Ello! Would there be a plantation near here?" Earless spoke, trying his best to be friendly.

The entire group turned as one to look at them, but no one said a word.

"Come on now, someone must speak proper English? Where do you live? Is there a plantation nearby? Someone be a good bloke and answer?" Earless asked, wondering if perhaps they had wandered upon a leper colony, as the group appeared quite ragged upon closer inspection.

The group still didn't speak, but growled in unison and rushed forward, swarming the pirates. The pirates fired their muskets and struck several of them, but it had no effect.

Earless now knew what they faced—zombies. He had sailed around Haiti enough to have heard stories of the living dead, but had thought them as much a myth as the Kraken. Now in one day, he had learned he was mistaken about both.

Charley let out a horrible yell as one of the zombies began to chew the entire side of his face off, ripping and tearing his flesh and biting right through the bone. More zombies swarmed him as he went down, ripping into his guts and tearing his intestines out as they feasted. Charley died with a gurgle as the zombies finally did enough damage to kill him.

The other pirates fared no better as they were all torn apart and eaten alive by the zombies. As Earless was pulled to the ground he saw a scene straight from Hell. Zombies were feasting on men's entrails, eating arms and legs as one would parts of a chicken. It was hard to tell by this point which body parts and internal organs belonged to which man, as the zombies were lost in the carnage and eating whatever they could find.

As Earless felt his shoulder being ripped apart he managed to draw his pistol and fire, blowing the top of the zombie's head off and killing it.

"Oh, so you have to kill the brain..." Earless said as the weight of the zombie he had killed pinned him to the ground. "I should have known that..." Earless said aloud as a zombie ripped his throat out and the warm blood spurted over his chest. He watched the moon as he was devoured, the sounds of his own flesh ripping and tearing in his ears as he breathed his last breath.

SEVEN

The next few weeks passed without incident for Shade. He didn't have any more experiences with the supernatural and none of the monsters had shown up yet. He had familiarized himself with the sheds and their content and had also learned to handle the generator. He also figured out the computer system and what he needed to do regarding paperwork. It was tedious but thankfully not too hard to figure out.

He had basically been doing the job of an everyday game warden. He did routine patrols through the swamp and kept an eye on the waterways and wildlife. So far he had only seen run-of-the-mill Georgia fauna. Squirrels, deer, raccoons, possums, and tons of birds had been around, as well as the slimier swamp denizens. He had seen several large alligators, but nothing large enough to cause alarm. There were also a lot of snakes in the area, mostly non-venomous water snakes, but water moccasins were also plentiful and he'd also encountered a few rattlesnakes on some of his outings on foot and on the ATV. Frogs and lizards were everywhere, including in the office, as he constantly found himself throwing chameleons and toads back out into the swamp. His biggest issue so far had been the damn bugs. The mosquitoes and gnats made things intolerable, and even though he used the best bug spray money could buy, and also the most scientifically advanced equipment to keep them under control, they still were ridiculous.

Shade alternated his time between staying at his own apartment and at the office apartment, and he was gradually becoming comfortable with the schedule. Waya still came by, but not every day as he had at first. The job had become fairly routine, and Shade was starting to enjoy it. This was what being a game warden had always meant to him. He even got to do some fishing under the pretense of taking measurements and tracking the fish in the area, although the black swamp wasn't tracked as closely as a normal fishing area.

So far, Shade had never had any trouble finding his way back to the office, so there must have been at least some truth in Waya's speech about him being chosen for the job. What had surprised Shade most was that he had found a few hunters and fishermen in the area.. He had asked them how they had found the place and they had all started in different areas and had somehow ended up in Black Swamp, with none of them understanding how. In every case, Shade had offered to take the people back to their vehicles in his own truck, including towing boats when necessary. He had used an excuse about toxic gas leaks to get them out of the swamp, and so far no-one had argued. Shade reckoned they all found the swamp a little creepy anyway, and were happy to get the hell out. Shade was just happy they had all survived, and marveled at how none of them knew just how lucky they were.

Waya had also showed Shade around the normal fishing and hunting areas nearby, and from time to time he would work his shift there. Shade felt much less pressure when he didn't have to constantly be on the lookout for the next bad event, so he liked getting to work in the mundane areas. Waya would sometimes swap shifts with Shade and work in the Black Swamp from time to time. He didn't want to lose touch with the place, or let himself forget how dangerous it could be.

One morning when Waya was working the non-haunted swamp areas, he pulled up in his pickup truck and had someone with him. Shade happened to be out on the dock casting for fish when they pulled up, and he watched as Waya got out of the truck, and then his companion.

Stepping out of Waya's truck was the most beautiful Native American girl Shade had ever seen. He didn't even try not to stare as they both waved and began to walk towards him. She was very petite, maybe five feet tall at most, and weighed maybe a hundred and ten pounds soaking wet, but she was very well put together. She was busty with a slim waist, and even with her short stature, her legs were long and toned. She was wearing cut-off shorts and a man's shirt tied above her stomach, showing off her flat belly and pierced belly-button. She had on high moccasin boots and her jet-black hair was in twin pigtails down past her shoulders on either side of her head. It was basically the same hairstyle Waya had, but to Shade it looked much better on her. Her skin was olive-toned, her cheekbones high, and her nose was very narrow. She smiled and her teeth were very white against her full lips. Shade couldn't take his eyes off of her as she and Waya walked onto the dock.

"All right, put your damn tongue back in your mouth and stop with the damn staring, your eyes look like they are about to pop the hell out," Waya said, Shade's ogling very apparent to him. He turned to the girl, "See, I bet you did this on purpose, I told you we were coming to the swamp and you dress like a damn porn star."

Shade broke his stare and laughed as the girl laughed too, Waya glancing back and forth between them, exasperated.

"Oh yeah, laugh at the old man. Shade, this is my daughter, Willow, and even though she dresses like a total tramp, well, it's because she is one," Waya said, although this time he was also laughing.

"Dad, stop it. Shade, just call me Awunkatunka, everyone does." Willow said, stretching out her hand for a shake. Shade frowned but did shake her hand.

"Um, okay, nice to meet you Awunk...Awuanka...I'm sorry, how did you say that?" Shade asked, perplexed.

"She's screwing with you, dumb ass. Just call her Willow, that's her real Cherokee name. That other name is some shit she made up," Waya said, getting a little tired of the situation already.

"Hello Willow, nice to meet you," Shade said, really meaning it. He tried not to be obvious as he checked her out. "So Waya, I don't remember you mentioning a daughter?"

"That's because I didn't, you horndog. She has been begging to meet you and I keep putting her off, but she finally wore me down and here she is. And by the way, don't rob the cradle. She's way too young for you."

"I'm twenty-eight!" Willow interjected.

"Damn, Waya, you have a twenty-eight-year-old daughter? But aren't you like, two hundred years old or something? That Cherokee blood runs hot, huh? Aoooga!" Shade said, having more fun then he'd had in a long time.

"Cherokee blood runs hotter than you know," Willow said, giving Shade a wink.

Shade winked back, "Maybe you can show me some

time."

"Hey, I'm standing right here! Willow, go wait in the truck, mosquitoes are gonna eat you alive dressed like that out here, you know we have to get going soon," Waya ordered.

"Well, okay. Shade, I hope to be seeing you around." Willow said, blowing him a kiss as she walked back to the truck, being sure she did the most exaggerated sexy walk ever.

"Oh, I hope so too. You have a good day now." Shade said, tipping his hat to Willow as she walked away.

Waya shook his head as she walked off. "She's really a good girl. She's just playing with you. She loves aggravating the hell out of me."

"Yeah I kinda figured that, I didn't mean any harm I was just playing along."

"I know, I know. But she's had a rough few years. She was married to a real asshole—drunken Indian that didn't do anything but slap her around. She wanted children but couldn't bring herself to have any with that bastard. One day she came home with a black eye and busted lip, so I casually went over and told him they were getting a divorce."

"How casually did you tell him?"

"My hand still aches from where I broke it when it gets cold."

Shade nodded, "I can't say I wouldn't have done the same."

"Anyway, he disappeared and she's been living with me and her mother the last few years, but she's gun shy. That flirting she just did with you was the most words she's spoken to a man since she got rid of that shit-eating husband of hers."

"Really? With a smokin' little body like hers I thought they'd all be lining up at your door," Shade said, needling Waya now.

"Dammit, Shade, stop that. Don't make me regret introducing the two of you."

Shade acted appalled. "Why sir, are you trying to set me up? I do declare, I think you want me for a son-in-law! Gimme a hug pops!" Shade reached out and tried to give Waya an exaggerated hug which he barely avoided.

"Now stop that. It's just we had her late in life, and I worry about her after we're gone. I don't know what motive I had for bringing her over. I guess I just wanted her to see there are still good men left in the world."

Shade was genuinely touched. "I'm glad you think I'm one of the good ones."

"Oh no, I meant myself, I brought her here to show her what an asshole you were in comparison," Waya grinned as he walked back to the truck.

Shade laughed, "Get the hell out of here, you useless old man."

Shade asked Waya later what had made him bring his daughter into a place as dangerous as the swamp just for an introduction. Waya just said he had gotten a feeling that Shade needed to meet her, and it was urgent, so urgent to even risk the swamp. The two of them hadn't spoken any further on the subject.

Waya waved as he got into the truck and Willow leaned out the window and waved back. Shade returned the wave as he watched them drive off. This was as happy as he'd been since returning to the States. He smiled as he cast his lure back into the water. He had no way of knowing how bad things were about to get.

Another few weeks passed by quietly. Waya had brought Willow over to see Shade a few more times when he wasn't working the Black Swamp, and the three of them had spent a lot of time together. Shade was even eventually invited over to dinner at Waya's house, which Shade enjoyed. Waya's wife was a very nice lady and an excellent cook. They had Mexican food and the four of them played cards afterward. Shade and Willow were starting to be drawn to one another, but both of them were slightly damaged for different reasons. Willow was still trying to get over her failed marriage, and Shade still hadn't completely dealt with his PTSD, but the two of them were good for one another.

Along with being a powerful shaman, Waya must have also been well-versed in human nature. He had thought that his daughter and Shade could both help one another get through the tough times in their lives, and so far he was right. Shade and Willow went on a few dates as the months passed, but the relationship still stayed mostly platonic. For all of the heavy flirting, and even though the two were physically attracted to one another in a magnetic way, they had kept things simple. Neither of them were ready for the next step yet, but they were still happy spending time together. Willow had made it fairly clear she wanted to take things very slowly, and Shade had no issues with this. Waya hoped nothing would happen to tear them apart, but for some reason he had a sense of foreboding about something.

Moe Stringer was a loser. He always had been and always would be. He sat in the parking lot in his SUV and watched the bank as he waited on his partners to emerge. Moe had met Randy, Richard, Eddie and Bones in the army. They had all been court martialed for slaughtering a village full of Afghan refugees who'd had no proven connection to terrorism. Moe and his four friends had only been able to enlist once the government had eased restrictions on convicted criminals in the armed forces. All five of the men had done time for various crimes. Armed robbery, drug trafficking, rape and murder, were nothing new to this group. Somehow they had all been thrown into the same group during the war in Afghanistan, and bad things had happened.

The five had managed to stay out of military prison because of a lack of evidence. That sometimes happened when most of the witnesses were dead. Rather than jail time, they had all been discharged, and since they all had similar interests, they had decided to stick together.

Their particular skill sets hadn't been much use to them back in the States, and even the extreme military contracting groups wouldn't touch them due to their hot potato status. Therefore, they had quickly found themselves broke. They had ended up in Savannah on their way down to Miami, hoping to hook up with some of Eddie's drug connections and find some gainful employment. However, some quick math had found them too broke to make it to Miami, and therefore some quick cash was needed. They decided to rob a bank.

Richard had some connections in gun running, so he had managed to procure some nice weapons for the group—an M16 for Randy, a 12 gauge assault shotgun for Eddie, and a Squad Automatic Weapon, or SAW rifle, for Bones. Bones had no need for such a large gun, but overkill was his thing. Richard had gotten an M16 for himself too, and since Moe was serving as driver, he had gotten a .50 caliber Desert Eagle Semi-Automatic handgun. The five men were useless human beings, but they knew how to use guns, and they knew how to kill people.

Moe heard gun shots inside the bank including the roar of the SAW rifle. Moe cursed under his breath and pulled the SUV directly in front of the bank, knowing that soon either his friends would emerge and need a ride, or they wouldn't emerge at all.

All four men came out, wearing ski masks, and dragging a female along with them. Given the situation, Moe barely had time to glance at her, but what he had seen he liked. The men all jumped into the car and Moe thought he heard screams coming from the back.

"Go, go, go! Just fucking go!" Randy said as he jumped into the passenger seat, and Moe wasted no time peeling out of the parking lot and onto the road.

Moe pulled directly into the traffic and the vehicle was met with the screeching of brakes and the honking of horns since he had no regard for the other vehicles. He pulled up onto the sidewalk, scattering pedestrians as he tore his way through the area. He knew the police would be along soon and their time was limited. Moe managed to get out onto the interstate before he heard the sounds of sirens in the distance. He glanced in the rear view to try to get a better look at the hostage sandwiched between Bones and Eddie, but all he could see was the dark hair on top of her head.

"Who's the guest?" Moe said as he weaved in and out of traffic.

"She's our back-up plan," Eddie said.

Bones, who hardly ever spoke, just grinned.

Shade was walking around the woods near the swamp, trying to see how high the water level was today when he heard what must be Waya's truck pull into the parking lot. Shade heard the engine roar and the brakes squeak as Waya was moving faster than usual. He heard the door slam and Waya began to call his name.

"Shade! Shade! Where the hell are you? Shade, get out here, dammit!" Waya called, running towards the office.

Shade ran from the woods and caught Waya as he was opening the office door. "Hey Waya, I'm here, what's up?"

Waya stopped, and ran towards Shade. Shade had never seen Waya in such a state. Waya seemed very upset and agitated and Shade thought he'd been crying.

"They have her, Shade! They have my Willow!"

After a few minutes of mostly incoherent rambling from Waya, Shade was able to calm him down and get him into the office, leading him to a chair and helping him sit. Shade was shaken now. He had never seen the usual stoic Waya this upset, and his anxiety was contagious.

"Now, slow down and start over, tell me everything from the beginning. A few more minutes aren't going to change this situation much, so let me know every detail you have," Shade said, taking a seat in the chair next to Waya and turning it to face him.

Waya took a deep breath and began to speak, "There was a bank robbery in downtown Savannah, down at the Georgia National Bank. It was four guys and they think there's a driver, so I guess five at least. These weren't your typical bank robbers—they were better organized, more dangerous. That's what the news said anyway, they showed some of the camera footage and talked to some of the survivors."

"Survivors?" Shade interjected, his stomach dropping as he heard the word.

"Yeah, they said one of the guys just snapped. He had some kind of big-assed machine gun and he just opened fire into the crowd for no reason. The bank was pretty full, Shade, he killed ten people, some of them women and children." Waya paused once again, rubbing his forehead in his hands, trying to rub the terrible thought right out of his mind.

"Waya, what's going on? Is your family all right?" Shade said, still expecting the worst, as he knew Waya wouldn't get this upset about a random bank robbery even if it did involve murders.

"They took her Shade. They took my Willow. They said they needed a hostage and they just dragged her out of the bank, kicking and screaming." Waya broke down into tears and Shade put a hand on his shoulder in sympathy.

"What can we do, Waya? What can *I* do? Where are the bank robbers now?" Shade asked. Shade wasn't sure exactly what Waya wanted, but Shade would be happy to take some guns from the armory and put these bastards in the ground himself if that's what Waya asked.

Waya regained his composure, pulling some tissues from the dispenser on the corner of the desk and wiping his face. "You don't understand. It gets worse. I think they're here, Shade. I think they are in the swamp."

Shade sat back in his chair stunned. "What the hell do you mean? How can they be here?"

"The cops lost them. They were chasing them in this area and they just disappeared. They disappeared right near the road that leads directly to this swamp. They are here somewhere Shade, I know it."

"But I didn't see anyone, Waya. Doesn't the road lead right to the office? Did you see anything when you drove in?"

"Shade you know how this swamp works. Just because they came down that road doesn't mean they ended up here. They could be on the other side of the swamp for all we know. All roads don't lead to the same places in the Black Swamp."

"How did they even find it though? The odds—"

"Shade, I think acts of violence and bad intent sometime lead people to the swamp. Sometimes people just end up here, other times they are drawn here like a magnet."

"But the fact that they took your daughter from the bank, and then ended up here? The odds on that would be astronomical!"

"Not if the swamp brought them here."

Shade once again found himself stunned at this new revelation. He had known the swamp could be an evil place, but he had never thought of it as sentient in any way. "What do you mean? Are you saying the swamp caused all of this?"

Waya shrugged, "I can't say for sure, Shade. But face the facts. I've been fighting this damn place for decades, I'm sure it hates me. If it wasn't for the little bit of hoodoo that I know, I would have been dead long ago, if I could even find the damn place to begin with. I think it's trying to get back at me through my daughter."

Shade turned towards the swamp, seeing it in a whole new way. "What about her mother, does she even know yet?" Shade asked, still watching the swamp.

"Yeah, her sister is over and a few of her cousins, she's handling it as well as she can, which is not too damn well."

Shade turned back to Waya, "So how far do you think this goes? Do you think the swamp led those guys to rob that bank and then led them here, or was it partially coincidence? How far can this damn place reach?"

"I don't know, Shade. I never really worried too much about this place as long as we stayed away from the general area. I never heard of anything like this happening. Hell, who knows, maybe I'm reading too deep into this and it was all coincidence, maybe they aren't even in the swamp. But I have a feeling they are."

Shade wasn't sure why, but he felt the same way, "Yeah, for some reason I agree with you. So what's the next step then? The longer they are out there, the more danger Willow's in." Shade didn't say it, but given the nature of the swamp, they both knew Willow could be dead already.

Waya glared at Shade with steel in his eyes. "The next step is we get a bunch of guns and kill those sons-of-bitches and get my daughter back. And if any monsters want to get in our way, we kill those bitches too."

Shade returned the steely stare, "Sounds pretty good to me."

EIGHT

"You piece of shit!" Moe yelled as he kicked at the door of the SUV repeatedly, denting it badly with each kick. "You damned piece of shit!"

"What the hell are you doing? Stop acting like an idiot and calm down," Richard said as he watched Moe attack the vehicle.

Richard had just finished dumping Randy's body in the woods near the road. The stress had gotten to Randy, and he had panicked. Richard saw his as a threat to the entire operation. So when the SUV had stopped, Richard told Randy to step out of the truck. He had then calmly put a bullet in Randy's forehead and hauled his body into the brush, leaving the weapon with the body, but dividing up his ammo as needed. He had left the gun as a sign of respect, feeling he owed Randy that much. The other men had barely batted an eyelash, just seeing it as more money to be split among themselves.

The men had been pursued by the police for several miles. They were forced off of the interstate and found themselves on back roads with the police still in hot pursuit. Robbing the bank was bad enough, but they figured killing ten people must have pissed the cops off, because they had been right on their ass the whole way. Moe had missed the turnoff that was mostly hidden by the woods, and thankfully the cops had missed it because once they turned onto the old dirt road the chase had ended immediately.

The road was very small and in terrible condition. It was also basically one lane, and Moe couldn't have turned around even if he had wanted to. The road didn't end, but turned to mud, and before they knew it, they were stuck, and stuck good. The SUV had bogged down in mud all way to the frame, and they all knew they had no one to free it.

The four men had pulled off their masks and were

standing around near the truck, talking. The hostage had kicked and fought so much they'd had to tie her hands with an electrical extension cord and cover her mouth with duct tape. Eddie had deep scratches on his face and Bones had a huge bite mark on his shoulder to attest to the ferocious nature of the hostage. Willow was currently sitting on the ground with her back against the tree eying the men with looks that could kill. Willow had been dressed casually in jeans, a t-shirt and tennis shoes, but even subdued it was obvious she was a knockout. Her Native American heritage was also clear enough that even the morons that had kidnapped her could tell her ethnicity. She had her hair in the usual long twin braids.

Eddie was short and stout, with long black greasy hair and pale skin. He appeared Goth, although he had done nothing to do so, it was just the way he turned out.

"That whore scratched the shit out of me!" Eddie said, rubbing the deep furrows on the side of his face.

"Oh quit whining like a little bitch, you don't hear Bones complaining," Richard said.

Bones had taken his shirt off and was so proud of the bite mark he wore it like a badge of honor. Bones was the exact opposite of Eddie, very tall and thin but still muscular. He was bald and his body, including his scalp, was covered in ugly prison tattoos he thought of as art. When Richard mentioned his name, Bones brushed at the bite like there was nothing to it.

Richard was the most appealing of the four, a clean cut guy with short blond hair and blue eyes who had practically movie star good looks along with a model's body. Richard could have gotten any woman he wanted, but instead he chose to rape them.

Moe was a common thug type, his body a combination of Bones' and Eddie's, as he was short like Eddie but skinny like Bones, a combination which pretty much made him a pipsqueak. He had long brown hair which he wore in a ponytail most of the time because he thought it made him cool. It made him look more like what he really was, a horse's ass.

The men had all brought along burner phones, but for some reason every phone had been busted in the crash, and not just broken, but literally destroyed. There was something supernatural about the way the phones had been destroyed, but these were the type of men who just wrote the incident off as bad luck and threw the broken pieces into the woods. The phones were broken, end of story. They didn't have time to contemplate the how or the why at this point.

"All right, here's the plan. The SUV is history. We need to grab the money and guns and head out through the woods here. I think we've ended up in a swamp so this shit isn't going to be fun. It's going to be downright unpleasant. We'll keep Pocahontas here along with us until we decide what to do with her," Richard said, playing the role of the leader as usual.

"Speaking of the little squaw, I think it's about time for some Custer's revenge," Eddie said with a slimy smile, reaching down to run his hand over Willow's thigh. She thrust her leg out, catching Eddie right on his knee and snapping it back with an audible pop. "Goddamn it, the little bitch just broke my leg!" Eddie screamed as he hopped around, bending his knee trying to make sure it wasn't broken.

"Then keep your greasy little hands off of her, you fat fuck! She's too good for the likes of you anyway," Richard said as he walked over and leaned down, getting as close to Willow as he felt safe, "but me however, well, me and Sacajawea here are going to get to know each other real well soon enough, aren't we sweetie?" Richard winked at Willow, but she still regarded him with as much disdain as a human stare could possibly contain.

Richard stood back up. "Anyway, let's get the guns and money together and get this show on the road, Johnny Law could pop his porky ass up here anytime."

The men all gathered at the SUV, splitting the money up into four separate paper sacks which they had brought along with them and also gathering their guns and as much ammo as they could easily carry.

Moe watched Bones sling his huge SAW rifle over his shoulder, not able to carry any extra ammo due to the size of the ammo boxes. "Don't you wish you had something a little easier to carry, like me?" Moe said, motioning down to the Desert Eagle in his belt.

"Bones can manage, don't worry," Richard said.

"Yeah but he doesn't have any extra ammo." Eddie said as he stuffed shotgun shells into every pocket he could find, and he was wearing camouflage pants with several large pockets, so he was able to carry a lot of shells.

"He won't need any," Richard said. Bones just nodded.

"All right gentleman, we're burning daylight, let's get this show on the road. Moe, Bones has got that big-ass gun to worry about so I want you to be in charge of the hostage. Please make sure she doesn't beat the shit out of Eddie anymore." Richard said, causing Eddie to huff and turn red like a spoiled child. "Oh, and also, did anyone happen to bring a compass?"

"I have one on my survival knife, but I think it's broken or something, it just keeps spinning around," Eddie said, holding the knife up so everyone could see the compass spinning like a dervish.

Richard turned his head to the side as he watched, "Hmm, I never saw one do that before. I bet your fat ass broke it."

Eddie once again whined, "Oh, come on, Rick why do you have to be so damned mean to me all the time?"

"First off, its Richard, not Rick, and I only pick on you because I like you Eddie," Richard said, before turning his back and whispering, "you big, fat, stupid piece of shit."

Moe looked up, "I think the sun sets this way so I guess that's west."

"As good a place to go as anywhere else, Joseph. Come on fellas, let's get going."

Moe walked over and stood in front of Willow, tapping the gun in his waistband, "You try any of that uppity shit with me, squaw, and I'll introduce you to Mr. Fifty Cal," Moe said, doing his best tough guy imitation. Willow responded by head butting him in the crotch, causing him to double over in pain and moan loudly.

"Oh goddamn it, can't you dumbasses do anything right?" Richard walked over and backhanded Willow across the forehead, slamming her back against the tree. He then kicked her in the side before she had even stopped moving. "Now, listen bitch, we aren't going to kill you yet, but I will beat the hell out of you if you don't calm the fuck down! You can still come out of this alive if you play it smart and not stupid, but this shit you're doing now won't be tolerated! Are we clear?" Richard said. Willow regarded him with the same disdain she had perfected on the others.

Richard turned to Moe who was still rubbing his crotch.

Richard shook his head and pulled Willow roughly to her feet, shoving her towards Moe. "Now watch her and stop being a dumbass!" Moe nodded and stepped behind Willow, pushing her forward to walk in front of him.

"Is everyone ready now? Eddie, have you had enough or do you want her to elbow you in the throat or something? Moe, how are those nuts, still tiny? Damn, why can't you all be like Bones? The quiet psycho type is so appealing. Now let's get the fuck out of here."

The men began their trek through the swamp, Richard up front with his M16 slung across his shoulder and his bag of money in his hand, Eddie right behind him, Willow being herded by Moe, and then Bones in the rear. They had no idea they were walking into Hell.

Shade and Waya had gone right into the armory to prepare for the hunt. Shade had gotten the M16 with the grenade launcher and decided his side arm was good enough for a back-up piece. Waya had gotten one of the thirty-aught-six hunting rifles with the scope and a small MP5 9mm submachine gun. He had also grabbed one of the combat shotguns with the pistol grip. He put his hand on one of the RPGs, debating whether to take it.

"I don't think we'll need that. I'll take some grenades," Shade said, tapping the grenade launcher.

Waya nodded and took his hand from the RPG, "That should be fine. Be sure you take plenty of grenades for the launcher. And let's take a few extra clips of silver for our side-arms. As a matter of fact, here, take this," Waya handed Shade a clip of silver bullets for the M16. "Don't load them up yet, and if you do, try to remember to only use single shots with those or they'll be gone in seconds. Then he added, "If we need those, I don't think we'll want them gone in seconds."

Shade nodded and put the clip in his flak vest. Both he and Waya were wearing them, more for the carrying space then protection, but these guys were packing big guns so it couldn't hurt to have both.

Shade jerked a thumb at the special weapons locker, "Do you think we'll need anything from there?"

Waya shook his head, "We'd have no idea what to take,

and besides we know our main quarry is human this time. We just aren't sure what we may have to go through to get to them."

"I don't think I had a chance to show you these yet," Waya said, handing Shade a black shotgun shell. "That's silver buckshot floating in a gel of what's basically holy water."

Shade held it between two fingers and shook it gently. The gel made a slight squishy sound. "Where the hell did you get that?"

"Same place I get all this other shit. I know a guy."

Shade glanced at Waya to see if that was humor, but he kept a straight face so Shade assumed that was the only answer he'd get. He handed the shell back to Waya who placed it in a box along with four others and put it in his flak vest pocket. "Let's hope we don't need that either."

As the two finished gathering their equipment, Shade voiced the obvious. "How are we going to find them? I mean thankfully we have plenty of daylight, but this swamp is pretty messed up, so how do we know where to go?"

"I can find them. Even in this swamp I can track most anything, especially anything human. Trust me, we'll get them eventually."

Shade was impressed with Waya's confidence, but also worried it was overconfidence. He assumed from Waya's sureness that he must have been in similar situations before, although not with the life of his only daughter at stake.

Once the two had finished preparations, they walked to the door, Waya in the lead. Waya stopped before going outside. "Shade, this swamp, I think there may be more to it then you realize. I don't think it's just a gateway to another side, I think it may be even more than that."

Shade tilted his head slightly, "What do you mean? I think we've been over this and nobody is sure exactly what the hell this place is..."

"I mean it's like this place draws its evil from the human psyche. I mean, it is one thing to see giant snakes and alligators—things that are at least based in nature. But when ghosts, vampires, and other monsters start showing up, I dunno, I think there's something else going on. One time we even got reports of a guy in a hockey mask carrying a machete. It's like the place reaches into everyone's minds and pulls out the nightmare creatures it finds. Maybe it generates them somehow, I'm not sure. Who knows, maybe all the mythical monsters of legend came right from this damn hellhole. My point is, don't be surprised by anything you see out here. There are weirder things than giant bugs to be found."

Shade listened to what Waya was saying, and it made the swamp feel even more sinister than it had before, something Shade wouldn't have thought possible. There was no telling what he could run into out there, or more importantly, what the bastards that had Willow could run into.

"I understand, Waya, now let's go get those sons-of-bitches." Shade said. Waya nodded and the two walked outside. They headed over to the boat and stopped, looking from the boat to the shed and back.

"ATVs or boat, Waya? You know better than I do," Shade asked.

"Let's take the boat. As much as I'd like to have the ATV, we can mostly walk where the ATV would take us. There's no way we can swim around here."

Shade nodded and they got into the boat. Waya started it up and drove out into the swamp as if he knew where he was headed.

"Are we operating within the law here? Should we have called the FBI or at least the State Patrol or something? I know we have the same authority as the police, but this might be out of our league." Shade asked as they sped through the dark water.

"We have certain, let's call them, *provisions* when things like this happen. We are authorized to do whatever it takes to bring criminals in when they get lost in this swamp, up to and including deadly force. It was established by Presidential Doctrine a long time ago."

"How long ago?"

"Roosevelt."

"Franklin?"

"Teddy."

"Whew, way back, then."

"Yeah, believe it or not, Teddy Roosevelt came out here once. He didn't get to see any of the weird shit, but he saw some of the big gators and the snakes. He explored the Amazon and all you know."

"Yeah, he was a bad-ass from what I understand. Now, are you sure you know where you're going?" Shade asked, not wanting to sound condescending but wanting to be damn sure Waya wasn't going to get them lost and killed.

"Yeah, I smell those bastards. When something human comes out like this, I can smell them."

Shade once again wondered if Waya was joking, but he wasn't. Shade sat back in his seat with his M16 in hand and examined the other weapon bags in the bottom of the boat. He hoped they wouldn't need all those guns, but was glad he had them in case they did.

The ragtag group had not gotten far when it was obvious they were lost. They all suspected it at first, but now it was a fact. Richard tried to get his bearings but the trees were all the same to him. Several times they came upon large bodies of water they couldn't cross, and had to change directions. If Richard didn't know better, he'd think the damn swamp was herding them exactly where it wanted them to go.

"So magnificent leader, where the hell are we?" Moe asked, keeping his eyes on Willow and checking her out. She caught him staring and gave him a look with eyes that burned fire, so he gulped and immediately became interested in a bird in a nearby tree.

"I don't know, dumbass, it's too bad I wrecked the SUV. Oh wait, that wasn't me. That was you, you dumb motherfucker!" Richard lifted his fist to strike Moe, causing Moe to holler and raise his arm to keep him from striking him, but Richard never followed through.

"It was an accident, you saw! You all saw!" Moe said, staring at the group and trying to get some backup. None came.

Willow used the argument to run, trying to make her escape even though her arms were tied and her mouth was duct-taped. She didn't get far as Bones reached out with one of his long arms and a speed that didn't fit his frame, and grabbed one of her pigtails, slamming her hard to the ground as she tried to run past him. The breath was knocked out of her and she lay on the ground gasping for air through her nose.

"Hey! Go easy on the merchandise!" Richard said,

walking over to Willow. "You really need to stop these silly antics of yours. If you keep it up we may have to hurt you. You'd still be able to walk fine with a few broken fingers, so keep it up and I'm going to let Bones snap a few of them."

Willow turned her gaze up to Bones, who grinned down at her, the huge machine gun still balanced on his shoulder as he blew her a kiss. She turned her gaze away from them and rolled to her feet as Eddie grabbed her by the shoulders, being sure to keep out of range of her kicks or a head butt.

"Good girl. Now, we need to keep moving. Eventually we've got to find something resembling civilization," Richard said, taking the lead once again.

"Moe, Richard told you to watch her, so watch her!" Eddie said, pushing her towards Moe who grabbed her by the upper arm and pushed her in front of him. Willow saw the large survival knife Eddie was carrying, and knew if her hands were free she could grab it and kill at least one of the men, but then she knew the others would shoot and kill her before she could take two steps. She had to do something, but what? She knew the best thing to do right now was to wait for an opportunity and see what presented itself. She also knew there was no way she'd allow herself to be raped. They'd have to kill her if it came to that. She wondered exactly where they were. She was hoping it was one of the swamps her father worked in, but things had happened so fast she couldn't be sure. *Just give me a chance, you bastards. Just one chance.*

NINE

THE MODERN ERA

    Jim and Bo drove their boat deep into the swamp, not knowing exactly where they were but not really caring. They had a GPS to get them home if they got lost, but right now they weren't even thinking about getting home. The two had decided to go out and try their hand at alligator hunting, just like that reality TV show they both loved so much. They weren't exactly sure what the laws were, concerning hunting gators in the state of Georgia, but they didn't care. This was just for the pure fun of it. They had made a huge treble hook and attached to a thick chain, and they were planning on hooking a few gators and having some fun. They had also brought Jim's twelve-gauge shotgun along to kill the gators once they got them up to the boat. Then they'd take the gators home and skin them, and cut the tails up for meat. They knew they wouldn't be able to legally sell any of the gator, but this was about bragging rights and being the king of the swamp. Jim and Bo had not decided which of them would be the actual king of the swamp, so they would need to share the title. That was okay—the swamp was big enough for two kings.

    As they sped deeper and deeper into the swamp, everything changed. When they had first entered the swamp, everything was pretty bright and green. Now for some reason everything was black. The water itself was now pitch black, and even though the two of them had been all over the swamps of Georgia, none of this seemed familiar. No matter, they were here to kill gators, and by God they were going to kill some gators. They found it unusual that they hadn't seen any gators yet, but they were sure some would pop up soon. Neither of them stopped to think that it was winter time and the gators would be hibernating. At least, in a normal swamp they would be.

Bo toyed with the shotgun as Jim drove the boat. "Hey Jim, why you reckon them boys on that show use rifles and handguns and never use shotguns to kill them gators?"

"Cuz they ain't as smart as us, I reckon," Jim answered.

"Yeah, I reckon you's right. We is pretty smart fellers," Bo replied.

"Yep, that we are," Jim agreed.

"Oh shee-it, Jim, look at them bubbles, I think that may be our first gator!"

Jim slowed the boat down as huge bubbles rose to the surface in the center of the channel. This was one of the wider waterways in the swamp, like a small river. The bubbles were much larger than any bubbles the two had seen in the water before.

"Damn he must be big! That might be some kinda record!" Jim said as he piloted the boat to the bubbles, turning the motor down to idling speed so they didn't scare the gator away. "Bo, get that hook ready and I'll get the shotgun ready, I think this is it."

Bo stood up and leaned over the side of the boat as Jim turned the motor off and let the boat drift. The water wasn't moving very fast so the boat was staying somewhat stationary in the channel. Jim grabbed the shotgun, a pump action, and held it at the ready.

Bo glanced at Jim, "Now when I hook him and pull him up to the side, you're gonna have to shoot him pretty fast." Bo secured the end of the chain to a fishing rod holder that was bolted onto the side of the boat. That way even if he lost his grip on the chain, the gator wouldn't be able to get away.

The bubbles were still rising right at the side of the boat, some of them as large as the fifteen-foot craft itself. "Damn, Bo, those bubbles are too big. I bet that's just a gas pocket or something down under the water," Jim said as he watched the water boil.

"I don't smell nothin'. You could be right but at least let me check it out." Bo swung the hook into the water, letting it drop a ways before he began to jerk it up quickly. He stopped as the hook caught on something, the weight of the object bringing his pull to a complete stand still.

"Damn, Bo, you got a log or something?" Jim asked,

seeing Bo had stopped pulling the chain.

"I guess that must be it, or maybe there's a damn old sunk boat or something under there," Bo said as he tugged on the chain, moving the boat but not budging whatever he had hooked. "Damn, now how do we get our hook out?" Bo asked, stopping and just holding the chain a second as he thought.

With no warning something snatched the chain through Bo's hands, the thick chain slicing his skin and cutting his fingers to the bone. "Ahhh, dammit! I just cut my damn hands up!" Bo yelled as the chain was rapidly snatched from the boat.

"Why the hell didn't you wear gloves?" Jim asked, neither man reaching for the chain as it rapidly reached its' end.

"They never do on TV. Why should I!" Bo said as he examined his bloodied palms.

Jim watched the chain as all of it was dragged into the water, "Hey Bo, don't you think you should--"

Before Jim could finish the chain pulled tight and the boat took off like a shot, pulled along by whatever was hooked under the black water. Both men yelled and fell back into the boat as they were pulled all over the river, moving as fast as they had with the motor running.

"Damn Jim, what the hell! Do you think we hooked a submarine or something? No way in hell that's a gator!" Bo said as the boat was pulled all over the channel.

"Hell if I know!" Jim said, still holding the shotgun and laying on the bottom of the boat, not trying to stand yet.

"The water was pretty still on top, but I'm not sure. What should we do?"

"Let's just ride it out, maybe the hook will come loose or something."

The two men just sat in the boat as it was dragged deeper and deeper into the swamp, stopping when it reached what appeared to be a lagoon. The boat stopped moving as fast as it had started, and just floated in the still water. Both men cautiously stood up. Even with his injured hands, now wrapped in a dirty rag from the tackle box, Bo pulled on the chain, testing it, but it was very loose.

"I guess the hook came loose," Bo said as he pulled the chain up from the dark lake. "Now what the hell do you think that was all about?"

"I don't know, but it was kinda scary, weren't it?" Jim said.

"Yeah, it sure were. I don't know what the hell that was, but--"

Before Bo could finish his sentence, the waters of the lagoon violently exploded, and the head of the largest crocodile either man had ever seen, broke the water. The men weren't even sure what they were looking at because the proportions of the beast were just wrong. The head of the animal alone was bigger than the entire boat. They both screamed as the beast's huge jaws opened and the monster bit the boat in half, Bo and Jim managing to narrowly miss being eaten as one fell to the back of the boat and the other fell to the front. The aluminum boat was ripped in half with a loud crunching of metal, and the men found themselves floating in the black water of the swamp as the creature disappeared from view, leaving the twisted pieces of the boat floating on the surface momentarily before they began to go under.

"Holy shit, Jim, what the hell was that? I think it was a —" Bo's sentence was cut short as he was swiftly sucked under the water and completely disappeared from view. Jim, still holding the shotgun, turned and swam to the bank. He swam as if the devil himself was on his heels, because that's exactly what was going on. He didn't want to let go of the gun so he fought with it as he dog paddled to shore, the black water darker than ever as he expected to be crunched between the monster's jaws at any second.

Jim did manage to reach the muddy bank, pulling himself up out of the water and onto the marsh. The mud was too viscous to walk in, and when he tried to stand he couldn't get his footing and sunk down to his knees. He clawed his way through the mud, throwing the gun to the side as he pulled himself along on his hands and knees, the sight of the hideous beast spurring him on to physical feats he may not have normally accomplished. He couldn't resist stealing a look back and saw the pieces of his boat sinking further under the water, the life jackets floating to the surface as the heavier pieces sank. Jim couldn't be sure due to how dark the water was, but he thought he saw crimson tinges in the black liquid which had to be Bo's blood. There was no sign of Bo himself.

Jim turned his head away from the water and tried to scramble his way to safety through the grass, but before he could get any further, the water right near the bank erupted again and the giant crocodile snapped at him, the loud grunt of the creature alone making Jim piss his pants. However, the crocodile had misjudged its attack and mostly missed Jim, managing to catch only one of his legs in its huge jaws. Jim screamed and grabbed the shotgun which was now buried in the mud nearby and began to strike the creature with it, using the butt of the gun as a club, but it only bounced off the armored head of the creature over and over.

The crocodile attempted a death roll, trying to take some of the fight out of his prey. Jim screamed again as the monster twisted his leg at a terrible angle, breaking it. The force of the roll caused Jim's leg to slip out of the monster's jaws, as his leg was small in comparison to the huge mouth of the reptile. Jim used this opportunity to aim the shotgun right at the creature's eye and fire. *Click.* The mud had obviously gotten into the gun mechanism and covered the firing pin or disabled it in some other way. Jim ejected the shell, mud dripping out of the magazine as the shell hit the ground. He aimed and fired again. *Click.* It was no good. The gun wasn't going to fire.

By this time the croc had backed into the water and was preparing for another attack. Jim drew the gun back like a baseball bat, preparing to swing as the monster charged again. The monster opened its jaws just as Jim swung the gun. It passed harmlessly through the scaled horror's open mouth. Jim stared directly down the throat of the beast as the smell of rotting meat wafted from the creature's maw. Jim didn't have to time scream or get a final curse in as the jaws snapped down on him, crushing him and sawing him in two. The creature shook its head, grinding its jaws down as it chewed Jim up and swallowed before sliding black down into the dark water.

Jim and Bo were obviously never seen again. People that knew them weren't surprised, because when the two had said they were going alligator hunting most people knew there was no way that was going to end well. Everyone assumed they had either gotten drunk, wrecked the boat and drowned, or maybe had an accident with the shotgun as neither man was known for following rules of safety. The idea that an alligator had eaten them had also been mentioned, but no one took that too seriously.

TEN

Waya was piloting the boat through the swamp like he knew his destination, so Shade just stayed quiet and let Waya lead. Shade wondered if perhaps Waya had some type of supernatural ability to track things down, as he followed some type of sixth sense that Shade couldn't figure out. After about an hour of riding in the boat, Waya pulled it up to a nearby bank and let it drift to a stop, bouncing against the dirt.

"Here. We need to go on foot from this point," Waya said as he switched the engine off. Shade didn't argue and grabbed the mooring line, jumping onto the bank and securing the boat to a nearby tree. Waya stood up in the boat and did some chanting, moving his hands in some strange gestures as he completed some type of ritual. When he had finished he said to Shade, "It's a spell of protection, something to make sure the boat is still here when we get back."

"Is that going to be enough?" Shade asked, skeptical.

"Along with this it will be."

Shade watched as Waya took two vials from his pocket and began to sprinkle the contents all over the boat and into the water, onto the bank and even on the tree to which the boat was moored. "Salt and silver dust, it will take care of whatever my chant doesn't."

Shade nodded, feeling uneasy about leaving the boat, regardless of the safety measures taken. Each of them grabbed a bag, Shade keeping his M16 ready and Waya choosing the hunting rifle as they prepared to track the dangerous criminals. Both men had brought bottled water, but no food. They didn't plan on being out here long enough to get hungry. Waya also took out his knife and made several large slashes in the tree for identification, once they needed to find their way back. He also stuck a reflector on the tree just in case, but hoped he wouldn't need to use it as he wanted to be back long before dark. Even though both men brought along flashlights neither relished the idea of being this deep in the swamp once the sun went down.

Waya stopped and closed his eyes. He took a deep breath, smelling the air. He then opened his eyes and pointed. "That way. Let's go." Shade followed without question, realizing he had no other option anyway.

"Waya, I brought four pairs of handcuffs. We are going to arrest these guys and take them in, right?" Shade asked. "I mean, I assumed we can fit everyone into the boat if need be, they can lie down in the bottom on top of each other for all I care."

"If Willow is unharmed, we can take the men to jail. If she is not, I may just shoot them or leave them tied to a tree out here."

"Works for me," Shade said with a shrug as the two headed off deeper into the woods.

The group was very unhappy. Each man was still carrying his weapon along with his share of the money, and they had gotten nowhere. The bugs were eating them all alive and the humidity was stifling. So far they had seen nothing to indicate they were getting any nearer to actual people, and they were all getting worried now.

"Richard, I hate to bring this up, but do you have any idea where the hell you're going?" Eddie asked, trudging along through the mud as it sucked at his boots.

"No, I don't. Would you like to lead, Porky McPorkerson?" Richard said sarcastically.

"Hey now, words can hurt. Why do you always have to pick on me about my weight? You know I have a glandular condition," Eddie said, his voice one step away from being a whine.

"Oh, that's right, sorry Eddie. And besides that glandular condition may just come in handy," Richard said as they continued moving through the woods.

"How so?" Eddie asked, genuinely curious.

"If we get stuck out here too long, we can eat your fat ass first. I bet you'd keep us all alive for weeks," Richard said without a hint of humor.

Moe laughed and even the usually stoic Bones chuckled

as Eddie's face turned beet red, whether with anger or embarrassment no one was able to discern. Willow wasn't really paying attention, her only thought being how to get away from these jerks, but so far no opportunity had presented itself.

Richard stopped and stomped the ground. "Dammit, this is ridiculous! How big is this fucking swamp anyway?" By now it was late afternoon and sun was beating down into the swamp. Even though the canopy of trees kept most of the direct sunlight from getting through, it still made it hot as hell, heating the inside of the swamp up through a type of weird osmosis.

"Take a seat everyone, let me think a minute," Richard said as he took a seat on a nearby log.

Willow walked over and sat against a tree without prompting, carefully leaning her back against it and sliding down to keep herself from falling since her hands were still tied. The men watched her sit and then pretty much ignored her, each of them lost in their own misery.

Willow heard a voice from over her shoulder say, "They are bad men, you know."

Willow strained her neck, turning around to see who had spoken. Standing just beside the tree was a little girl, around ten years old. She was barefoot and wore a dirty white cotton dress. Her hair was long and blonde and matted. Her face was streaked with dirt as though it had been a long time since she'd bathed. Willow stared at her dirty hands and feet, wondering just where this little girl had come from.

She glanced at the men, not wanting them to see the girl out of fear of what they might do to her. She turned back to the girl with pleading eyes, waving her tied hands and nodding, trying to signal the girl to run, get away, hide, do something.

The girl stood there and stared at the four men, who had yet to notice her. Willow looked back and forth from the girl to the men and felt even more helpless than she had before. The situation was frustrating her to madness.

"They are bad men," the girl said again, giving the men a sour look. The girl then looked at Willow, as if noticing for the first time she was bound and gagged. "Did they do this to you? Do you need me to untie you?"

Willow nodded so vigorously she was afraid she'd strain her neck as the girl offered her a glimpse of freedom. The girl walked over and began to tug at the duct tape around Willow's mouth. *No, No, NO, not the tape! Get the hands first, untie my hands please. Don't let them see! Please, please, please...*

The girl managed to pull the duct tape from Willows mouth, leaving her face red and burning as she snatched it away. "There we go, now we can talk. I hope that didn't hurt too badly. I wasn't sure how else to get it off."

Willow shushed the girl quietly, trying to get her to whisper. The girl had been speaking in a normal tone of voice, but so far the men still had not so much as glanced in their direction. "Shh, you have to whisper! Now get my hands, please!" Willow pleaded, watching the criminals as she held her hands up to the girl, hoping she would be strong enough to loosen the cord knotted around her wrists.

The girl began to tug at the cord, not being able to loosen it much as her small hands pulled at it. "What's your name? My name is Meg. Do you live around here?" the girl said, working at the cord way too nonchalantly for Willow.

"My name is Willow. Please hurry!" Willow said, frantically working her wrists together and trying to pull them free.

"Hey! Who the hell are you talking to?" Moe said, and Willow's heart dropped as she saw him heading her way. She shut her eyes tightly and was unable to stop the tears that flowed down her cheeks. She had been so close. Now they would have two hostages—and who knows what they would do the girl?

"How the hell did you get the tape off?" Moe said, seeing the tape crumpled up and tossed to the side. Willow just kept her eyes shut tightly, trying to imagine she was anywhere but there. "Dammit this tape is ruined. Hey, did anyone bring the duct tape along?" Moe called to the group, but everyone shook their heads. "Dammit! You listen good, little girl. If you make one sound, one peep, I'm going to kill you and we'll just have to go without a hostage. This thing has turned into one big cluster anyway, so I'm beginning to think you're more trouble than you're worth. Are you even listening to me? Open your eyes, bitch!" Moe said, slapping Willow's cheek.

She opened her eyes and whispered, "I won't make a sound."

Moe nodded and smiled, like he'd imposed his will on

her. "There we go, that's a good squaw. Now sit there and shut up."

Moe turned and strutted off, hoping the other guys had seen the conversation but he was crestfallen to learn none of them had. Willow waited until he was talking to Eddie before she tried to find Meg. The girl was gone, and Willow could only wonder how she had managed to disappear so quickly.

Waya traveled confidently through the swamp as Shade followed right behind him. From time to time they would begin to sink into the mud, their boots making a sucking sound as they pulled them free. Once the mud was too deep Waya would veer in a different direction and always find solid ground. Shade was one of the elite of the elite, and he had trained and served with the same, yet he had never seen anyone move like Waya. When you factored in Waya's age, it was amazing. This was Shade's first time seeing Waya in action, and Shade realized Waya was a different breed.

The two had seen the usual swamp life: gators, snakes, frogs, turtles, and various birds and mammals, but they had yet to see anything out of the ordinary, and the pair was grateful. Shade wasn't sure how the outlaws would react if they heard gunfire or explosions, and given the stillness of the swamp, any loud sounds would travel a great distance. They had discussed things during the walk, and decided if they did encounter anything, they would try their best to avoid it rather than try to kill it and give their presence away. They also knew that might not be an option, as the things they were likely to encounter wouldn't be so easily avoided. A few times Waya did stop as if he heard something Shade didn't, freezing in place and motioning for Shade to do the same. Waya would hold a finger over his lips to indicate complete silence. Eventually, Waya would be satisfied and the two would continue on their way. Shade hadn't recognized anything out of the ordinary and wondered if Waya was hearing anything or just being cautious. This wasn't the time to bring it up anyway, so Shade just followed Waya's lead. Shade hadn't really given much thought to what he would do once they caught up with the kidnappers, but he knew his training would kick in automatically and he would do whatever needed to be done. He had hoped the days of killing men were behind him, but he was still cynical enough to know some men deserved killing. Anyone that killed ten innocent people and kidnapped a helpless girl? They were definitely 'some men'.

"Are we going in circles? 'Cuz it feels like we are going in circles," Eddie said, once again proving himself to be the biggest whiner in the group.

"You know, I really wish we could find a dairy farm out here somewhere, but I know the odds are against that," Richard said.

Eddie was puzzled, "What the hell do you want a dairy farm for?"

"So I can get you some cheese to go with that whine, you imbecile!" Richard said, as Bones smiled and Moe chortled.

Eddie was still puzzled. "I don't get it."

Richard shook his head, "Of course you don't."

The group continued on in silence, Willow keeping her mouth closed even though it was no longer taped. Even though the girl had worked at her hands, she was still bound tightly and there wasn't much she could do about that.

The group continued along in silence for a while before Moe spoke. "Hey guys! What the hell is that? Is that a tree house?"

Everyone turned to Moe as he pointed into the distance. The group turned as one to follow the point to something in a tree quite a way off. It did slightly resemble some type of tree house. It was about the size of a small one, but was a cylinder shape rather than a house shape. It was big enough for people to climb inside, especially children, but it was way up the tree, and appeared unsafe.

"I don't guess anyone thought to bring some binoculars?" Richard said as he squinted into the distance.

"Yeah, I have some of the little ones, hang on... Shit, they are in the glove compartment," Eddie said.

"Thanks, Eddie, we can always count on you," Moe said.

"Fuck you, Moe!" Eddie said, flipping him off. Richard had always carried himself as a leader, and as such Eddie was always intimidated by him, but Moe just came across as a flunky the same as Eddie, so he wasn't going to take the ribbing from an equal. Moe just laughed and flipped Eddie off.

"That could be a few things. Way out here in the swamp, there's a good chance that's a deer stand. If so, maybe the hunters left something in there we can use, such as water. If that is in fact a tree house, then someone's home could be nearby, or maybe even a neighborhood. Since we aren't exactly overloaded with options here, I say we head that way," Richard said, heading in the direction of the tree house in case anyone in the group thought he was putting it to a vote, which he had no intention of doing. The others had no better ideas either, so they followed Richard.

Willow had been keeping an eye out for Meg who she thought might be following them, but she had seen no sign of the girl. The kid knew the woods, though, so it was possible she was just out of sight. Willow strained her eyes to make out the tree house. It appeared to be a light gray color, the color of weathered wood, so there was a strong chance it was some type of unusual tree dwelling. *Could that be where Meg lives?* Willow couldn't help but feel uneasy as they neared the structure.

"You shouldn't go there," a voice said from right beside Willow. Willow was startled and couldn't help but scream as she saw Meg, a solemn expression on her face.

"Hey, what the hell are you screaming at? Did something bite you?" Moe said from his position directly behind Willow. Willow turned and glanced at Moe, scared for Meg now. As she turned back to Meg, she was gone, vanished without a trace. Willow searched around, trying to find the girl. *How did she move so fast?*

"Now what are you looking at? Is something wrong with you? What are you doing?" Moe said, and the others in the group wondered what was going on.

"I think a horsefly bit me," Willow said meekly, trying to divert the attention as quickly as possible. "I'll be fine."

"Suck it up, then!' Moe said as the other men turned their attention back on their path and once again ignored everything behind them.

Willow's uneasiness grew. There was something wrong with this place, the entire swamp just felt *wrong*. She had no idea what was waiting for them, but she just knew it wasn't good.

Shade and Waya kept making their way deeper and deeper into the swamp, on a random path, but the entire time Waya acted as if he had a direction in mind. Even Shade's excellent wilderness skills weren't doing him much good. This swamp just didn't behave the way it should. Shade could have sworn the landmarks were changing as they passed them. Every time he tried to get his bearings, he didn't recognize the area he had just passed through. He was stricken with a terrifying thought: *What if something happens to Waya and I have to find my way out without him?*

Shade shook his head to clear it of such thoughts and just concentrated on following Waya. This mission was too important to worry about things imagined—he had enough to worry about in the real world. Even when they found these thugs they would still have to figure out a way to get Willow away from them. That was if Willow was even still with them, the alternative being too horrible to contemplate.

Shade had also wondered whether the men had just let Willow go once they got a few miles down the road. For all he and Waya knew, Willow could be back at home with her mother already. They both had their cell phones and radios, but given the location, it wasn't like such devices were always reliable. All ramblings aside, Shade was fairly certain the girl was in the swamp along with the bank robbers. He was certain because Waya was certain, and Shade was learning to trust Waya's instincts.

They had been traveling through rough terrain for a while now, and even though Shade was in top shape, he was beginning to feel the humidity and the strain. Waya, however, appeared fresh. Shade wasn't sure how Waya stayed so spry at such an age, but he hoped to learn his secret. The two continued on, determined.

The group was able to keep the tree dwelling in sight as they moved in. There was a path leading to the area, which they all took as a good sign. A path meant something—hopefully people—used this area. They had no way of knowing that ahead of them, just out of sight, the grass and trees were parting just for them, as the swamp itself led them just where it wanted them to go.

As they approached the structure, a loud buzzing noise became audible. It sounded like some type of power tool, although it was hard to pinpoint exactly what the sound was, or from where it was coming.

"What the hell is that?" Moe said, as the buzzing got louder.

"I think we may be in luck, and that may be the sound of a power cable buzzing. You know, how the transformers sound sometimes?" Eddie suggested, giving insightful information for a change.

Richard clapped his hands together in mock applause. "Why, Eddie, I do believe you may be onto something there. That does indeed sound like something electrical, maybe even a large light of some type. That could mean we are approaching civilization, lady and gentlemen—and I do use the term loosely. Somehow I don't think you're a lady," Richard said, laughing at his own joke.

The others, including Willow, just ignored Richard's comment, as they were all intrigued by the thought of seeing people once again. Willow wasn't sure what they were going to do with her once they got out of this swamp, but this place was so creepy she wanted out regardless. They were very close to the structure now, and they all stopped to admire it.

It was larger than they had thought, and was bigger than most tree houses children built. It was a large, gray cylinder, very smooth and well-rounded. A large opening was at the bottom, a round hole that a man could easily have climbed inside, but nothing was in place to help anyone climb inside. Normally in a case like this, boards of some kind would have been nailed or tied to the tree to serve as a makeshift ladder. Perhaps the owners just brought a tall ladder along with them anytime they wanted to get inside? That would certainly deter any intruders, as the climb would be impossible otherwise. There was something about it that was familiar, but no one in the group could decide exactly what made it familiar.

"What the hell is that? I never saw a tree house like that."

Eddie said, scratching his ass as he looked up at it. He decided to go on ahead, going down the path as the others studied the structure.

"I've never seen anything like that either..." Richard said quietly, trying to put together just what his eyes were telling him about this unusual object.

"Hey, I know what it looks like!" Moe boasted triumphantly.

Before Moe could elaborate, he was drowned out by an increase in the buzzing noise. The group hadn't been paying attention since they had been so focused on the object, but the buzzing was now very loud, and be getting louder.

Something then emerged from the hole at the bottom of the structure. No one could quite make it out due to the sheer impossibility of what it was they were seeing. It crawled from the hole and began to crawl around on the side of the structure. Soon others climbed out, and within seconds the structure was teeming with the creatures.

They had wings and long bodies that were striped black and yellow, with six legs and a huge abdomen that ended in a huge stinger. There was no mistaking it. Hornets. The large structure was in fact what had to be the biggest hornet's nest on the face of the earth. The men didn't know it, but it wasn't the largest nest in the world. It wasn't even the biggest hornet's nest in the swamp.

By this point Eddie was nearly out of sight, as he had kept walking while the others had stopped to gawk at the large nest. Everyone watched in horror as on cue, the hornets swooped down, heading right for Eddie.

"Dammit, Eddie, look out!" Richard yelled, running towards Eddie, Moe and Bones running along after him.

Willow saw this as her chance. She prepared to bolt into the woods, but a voice stopped her.

"I wouldn't do that if I were you," Meg said, suddenly standing right behind Willow, who froze.

"What the hell are you?" Willow said, losing her patience with the strange little girl.

Gunfire erupted, startling Willow who turned to see the men now engaging the creatures in battle. Willow had only turned away for a second, but when she glanced back down the little girl was gone yet again. This time Willow wasn't even surprised, but she did wonder what she should do. The little girl had told them not to come this way, and she had been right. She had also told Willow not to flee. Willow was mentally reviewing her options when the choice was taken out of her hands. Hornets began to fly in her direction, so she ran towards the only source of protection she saw in the immediate vicinity—the men with guns.

Before Richard had even gotten halfway to Eddie, he saw one of the giant hornets land on him and begin to thrust its stinger into Eddie over and over as it flapped its wings and pulled Eddie to the ground. As Richard ran nearer, another hornet, and then another landed on Eddie, all of them stinging him over and over as Eddie screamed in pain.

Richard cursed and aimed his M-16 as he ran, firing off single shots with each one striking the hornet he wanted to hit. He heard loud buzzing behind him, and saw hornets flying down at him, but before he could even turn to aim at the new threat, Bone's SAW coughed and the hornets were cut in half. The sound of Moe's .50 caliber handgun also boomed through the air, as he carefully took aim and dropped several of the hornets. The large bullets of the two weapons were able to rip the large insects to pieces with a single shot, so the men were holding their own against the monsters.

Willow ran towards the men, in awe of how well they operated once the fighting started. They were incompetent morons, but now that they had something to kill, they were pure professionals. Even though she had been present in the bank when they had killed the innocent people, that had been like shooting fish in a barrel—basically an unskilled slaughter. This, however, was methodical, and the men were a well-oiled machine.

Willow crouched under a nearby bush and watched the battle unfold. She found herself torn. On one hand, she would like nothing better than to see her tormenters killed the vicious creatures. On the other, she knew that she stood a much better chance of survival if the men won this battle rather than the insects, so she decided to just stay quiet and deal with whatever result fate handed her. She contemplated running away again, but the loud buzzing of the insects and the sheer evilness they exuded, kept her glued where she was hiding. If she ran, she would surely die at the stinger of a terrible nightmare. If she waited, there was a least a chance she could survive. She decided to take that chance.

Richard ran over to Eddie, carefully firing single shots to kill the hornets and then kicking the carcasses away. By this point Bones and Moe were taking care of the insects so Richard could check on Eddie. It was already too late. Richard couldn't hide his disgust as the got his first good look at Eddie. The stingers on the beasts were so large they had made puncture wounds and it appeared as though Eddie had been stabbed several times. That alone would have killed him, but the real damage had been done by the venom. Eddie's entire body had swollen to twice the size of his already robust proportions, the skin stretched so tight around his bloated frame it was impossible to identify him. The face just wasn't Eddie. Froth poured out of Eddie's mouth and down his body as Richard tried to determine whether Eddie was still alive or already dead. The huge swollen body began to convulse, but Richard still wasn't sure.

Richard aimed the M16 right at Eddie's forehead and pulled the trigger, deciding to end Eddie's suffering. Whether Eddie was alive or dead was a moot point anyway, as they had no way to help him. Even if they had been right on the doorstep of a hospital, there wouldn't have been anything that could have helped him. Richard half expected Eddie's body to explode when he shot it, or deflate like a punctured balloon. It did neither, the bullet just passing into his brain no more or less violently than it would have any other human.

Richard then began the task of taking useful supplies from Eddie's corpse, starting with the shotgun and then working on the many pockets Eddie had packed full of items. The steady staccato firing of Bones and Moe taking out the insects had become background noise to Richard, so he was caught off guard when one of the hornets made it closer than the others, buzzing right by him and causing him to dive onto the dirt. Richard rolled onto his back as the hornet dove at him, stinger first. Richard just managed to get his gun up in time, firing several shots so that when the hornet did land on him it was just an empty shell, the stinger scraping harmlessly along his clothing. Richard saw a thin trail of liquid—venom from the monster. The amount of poison the creatures could inject was astounding, and Richard knew that even one sting would be fatal.

He saw Bones and Moe still killing the beasts with precision, but he also saw the number of hornets were legion. There was a good chance they would run out of ammo before they managed to kill all of these behemoths, and even if they did wipe them out, what if there was another nest out here? Just as Richard thought this, he heard the click of the SAW, indicating it was empty. Bones shrugged at Richard, tossing the now useless automatic rifle on the ground. Richard tossed him Eddie's shotgun, and Bones caught it and began to kill the monsters again, not missing a beat.

Richard began to rifle through Eddie's pockets again, now stuffing all of the shells into Eddie's money bag. This was more of a boon than a tragedy in the men's eyes. With Eddie gone, they had more money to share and it wasn't like he meant anything to them. Richard took Eddie's survival knife, stuffing it in the bag. He stuck his hand in another of Eddie's pockets. *Is this what I think it is?* He thought. He stuck his hand deeper, and was rewarded by finding another. Eddie may have just saved them all.

Richard stood up, tossing the bag containing the shotgun shells at the feet of Bones, who by now needed to reload anyway. "Bones, load up and aim at the very top of that damn nest, I think that shotgun should have that kinda of range. I need you to bring that motherfucker down!"

Bones nodded as he reloaded, trusting Richard's judgment. As usual, Moe wasn't quite as trusting.

"Bring the nest down? Damn, Rich, that's gonna send every one of the bastards after us! Who knows how many are in that thing?" Moe said as he kept picking his shots and killing the bugs. Richard had thought Moe was stupid for carrying so many spare clips, but now he grudgingly had to admit Moe was right for doing it.

"Trust me and quit whining like a bitch! Do it Bones," Richard said, eyeing the nest as Bones aimed the shotgun right at the top of it, just where it was attached to the tree.

The shotgun spit fire over and over, the buckshot tearing through the nest. Richard knew the nest was made of paper, and although he was sure it was much stronger than a normal hornet's nest, he didn't think any paper could hold up against buckshot.

The buzzing got louder and louder as the paper was torn by the shells, the nest starting to droop a bit. Richard knew they needed to bring the nest down fast. Once the hornets knew the entire nest was threatened, they would come swarming out and overwhelm them.

The nest slid further down the tree, now hanging by only one wide strip of paper. Richard was using his M16 to help cover Bones and Moe had been helping, but the hornets were getting agitated and more of them were emerging. Just as Bones aimed to make the shot that would hopefully bring the nest down, the shotgun clicked on empty. Bones went into the bag to reload as Richard cursed, flipping the M16 to full auto and using the rest of his clip to shred the paper holding the nest up.

The nest dropped as the men scattered before it. It hit the ground and bounced, the buzzing so loud now it was painful. But now Richard was ready. Even before the nest had stopped rolling from its fall, Richard ran forward, pulling the pin on one of the grenades he had gotten from Eddie and tossing it as hard as possible into the nest opening.

"Fire in the hole!" Richard yelled, diving as the other men did the same, honed from their years of military service. Willow was still hidden under the bush as she watched the entire scene unfold, but she crouched into a ball and covered her head with her arms and hands, being sure to shield her ears.

Instead of a loud explosion, it was a subdued *WHOOSH* as the grenade exploded deep inside of the nest. The buzzing stopped immediately. Richard hadn't been sure how the nest would react to the grenade. He half expected the paper to just disintegrate and the force of the explosion injuring them all, but it was the exact opposite. He realized then just how many more hornets must have been inside the nest. The sheer mass of the hornets must have absorbed most of the concussion, keeping shrapnel within the confines of the paper hell. Richard popped a new clip into his M-16 and the three men casually picked off the last few hornets as the buzzing finally stopped. Willow saw this and tried to escape this time, but as she ran from the bushes Bones was ready for her, tripping her with his large leg and causing her to fall face first, hard. He put his foot on her back, holding her down as he helped kill the last few hornets.

Richard took out his butane lighter and walked over to the

nest, holding his flame against the paper. As expected, it went up pretty quickly, burning just the same as any dry paper.

"Damn, man, are you trying to burn down the whole forest?" Moe asked as he watched the nest start to ignite.

"Pretty much," Richard said, giving Moe a serious look. Moe just nodded, burning the place down sounded like a good idea to him.

Willow didn't struggle, just watched the nest burn. At least one of her captors had died, so her odds were better now. She didn't have time to worry about the giant hornets. Normally, something like that would have frightened her to no end, and probably changed the entire way she viewed the world. It most likely still would, but first she had to survive the human monsters.

"What the hell do you think that was all about? Mutants?" Moe asked, examining one of the dead bugs.

"It's gotta be. Some of that damn radiation or maybe some chemicals. I had no idea that shit could really happen," Richard said, staring at one of the hornets. Bones was gathering shells together and reloading, making sure the shotgun would be prepared for their next battle. He still kept his foot firmly planted on Willow's back, holding her in place. Bones had a disassociation with reality that came in handy in this situation.

"So Eddie had a grenade?" Moe asked.

"He had two," Richard said, holding up the other one. "I'm going to hold onto it. I have a feeling we may need it. Come on, bring your bags over, let's go ahead and divide this cash up."

The men complied and split the money three ways. They finished going through Eddie's pockets, but other than some shotgun shells and a small six-shot .22-caliber revolver, no surprises were to be found.

"How many clips you got left, Moe? I have five for the M16 and six shots in this little pistol and I'm done," Richard stated.

"I have four clips, seven rounds each," Moe answered.

"Damn, Moe, how many clips did you have? You must have shot up five or six in that little battle."

"Hell, I used ten! But you know I'm a hoarder," Moe said, grinning.

"Did you say whorer?" Bones asked, actually making a

joke. The two men stared at him blankly, wondering if they were hallucinating, before both of them laughed.

"Damn, all it takes is the most dangerous battle of our lives and ol' Bones here turns into a comedian, who'd a thunk it?" Richard said, slapping Bones on the back.

Richard then turned his attention down to Willow, who had been completely ignored. "Glad to see you made it too, squaw girl. The two of us still haven't been properly introduced, if you know what I mean," Richard said, winking at her.

Willow gave him the best look of disgust she could muster as he started talking to Bones and Moe once again, making further plans.

"You were lucky this time, but you're all going to die here." Meg said, abruptly appearing beside Willow. She was standing right between Bones and Richard, only a few feet away from them both, and neither of them had any idea she was there. *They just can't see her. What the hell is she?* Willow thought as she blinked slowly. When she reopened her eyes, Meg was gone.

ELEVEN

Waya and Shade heard the shots in the distance, and even though they had yet to identify or even acknowledge it, they had also heard the buzzing. Shade knew how hard it could be to use sounds to judge direction and distance, and he had a feeling in this hellish place things were even less reliable, but Waya headed in the direction of the sounds, and Shade followed. The shots went on and on. Shade heard a large machine gun as well as more automatic fire and what sounded like random large bore single shots. The sounds were distant, so the men knew they had a ways to travel.

The gunfire went on forever, with the large machine gun eventually going silent, and a shotgun taking its place. There was still that strange droning, faint but there. Neither man knew what was going on, but it was some type of firefight and they both worried for Willow's safety.

Shade wondered if perhaps the police had caught up with the robbers and the weird buzzing was the sound of a siren in the distance, although that was unlikely. The gunfire did indicate a battle of some kind though, so Shade hoped someone would kill those bastards and get Willow out of there in the process.

Waya didn't speak, and Shade didn't want to push him, so the two walked along in silence, hoping to reach the battle in time to help. This was all starting to feel way too familiar to Shade, and also entirely unwelcome. He didn't need to have some sort of attack now—too much was riding on him. He took a deep breath to steady himself and followed tightly on Waya's trail.

The quartet continued on through the swamp. They had already been hot and thirsty, and the battle had only served to make them even more so. The gun smoke had also burned their eyes and noses especially Willow's, who had never been in the middle of such warfare. They all wanted water, but had found none suitable to drink.

The group was trudging through the wet ground, having to make a few detours as they were running into lagoons and other bodies of water, but found nothing fit to drink. They were moving through some very thick woods when they emerged onto a pretty wide trail. It seemed misplaced, a road right in the middle of the swamp.

"What do you think this is?" Moe asked, looking up and down the road.

"It's obviously some type of road, but if you mean do I know where it goes, the answer is no," Richard said, his tone condescending. He was beyond pissed off now and in no mood to mind his manners.

Moe didn't let it bother him—he was used to Richard by now. As the four stood in the center of the roadway, they heard something in the distance. They all paused and listened harder, wondering if their ears were playing tricks on them.

"Is that what I think it is?" Moe said, cupping his ear.

"It sounds like singing. Almost like church hymns," Richard said, and Bones nodded in agreement. Willow stared down the road in the direction of the church but didn't say a word. In her mind she could already see the three men slaughtering an entire church congregation in cold blood, and she wondered if there would be any way she could stop them.

"You all are still going to die," Meg said, once again appearing beside Willow out of nowhere. Willow regarded her with contempt. The child was just annoying at this point, and she was sick of her mean little quips.

"Go away," Willow said, turning her head away from the girl. When she turned back, as expected, Meg was gone.

"Did you say something?" Richard said to Willow.

"No."

"I thought I heard you mumbling something. Do you know anything about this singing we're hearing? Is there a church near here?"

"I don't know, I have no clue where we are," Willow said truthfully.

Richard shrugged and started down the road in the

direction of the singing. "That's our only option now, so let's go say hello to the nice church folk. If they're lucky we'll just steal a car and drive on out of here, and they won't even know we were around. At least, not until gramma finds out her car was swiped, but she better realize she's getting off easy."

Moe grabbed Willow by the arm and pulled her along, this time with Bones bringing up the rear. They continued down the road for maybe a mile and then the road dead-ended at a church. It was a small, weather-beaten, one-room church. The steeple wasn't very high but the cross was still sturdy at the top. There was a small graveyard behind the church enclosed by a low, rusty wrought iron fence. There were no vehicles around the church. Willow had especially hoped the men could find a car because at this point she would rather have been stuck with them in a car on the road rather than have an entire church full of people at their mercy. She had already given up hope on finding any real help at the church. She knew all she'd manage to do was get some innocent people killed.

The men moved in, stopping just at the edge of the churchyard. The church itself could have been a century old, or fairly new and just aged by the environment. This swamp could age anything quickly, so the church could have been built last week and already be weathered. They stood around listening to the hymns coming from the open windows of the church. There were no visible power or phone lines running to the church, and no lights were visible anywhere, so they assumed this was some type of primitive church that operated without electricity. It was also possible the lines were underground. They still weren't sure how close to civilization they were, so maybe there was a shopping mall right beyond the trees.

Willow considered her options. If she attempted to warn the people, she'd just get herself and a bunch of others killed. If she attempted to run, would they attempt to catch her at this point? They could surely gather hostages from the church if needed, so they may find her no longer worth the trouble and just kill her outright. In a way, she thought that may even be a relief. She decided to once again play it by ear and just go with whatever option left the least people dead, excluding her companions.

"All right boss man, your call. What now?" Moe asked,

keeping one hand firmly wrapped around Willow's bicep to keep her in place. Bones also turned to Richard, awaiting his orders.

"We can't just steal a car like I wanted to, but these are the only people we've seen since we got to this hellhole. They had to get here somehow, either they walked or maybe a bus picks them up or something. Either way, I think this is our ticket out of here. I think we should play this one cool though," Richard said as he glanced back and forth between the two.

"Here's how we play it. See those bushes over there? We're going to leave our guns and our bags right under them. Moe, you give Bones your pistol, he's the only one of us with big enough pockets to hide that big-ass thing. I'll take the little revolver, too. If we have to get rough, I think that's all we'll need with this crowd," Richard said, being sure his words were sinking in. Both men nodded in understanding.

"Now you," Richard said, rubbing the back of his hand along Willow's cheek, caressing her with mock affection, "We need to decide about you. I guess we could kill you now and leave your body out here; they'd never find you until we were long gone." Richard grinned evilly as Willow just stared at him defiantly.

"Or, we could untie you and you could mind your manners. I think having a little filly like you around may add to our story. Me and you are married, and we were camping with our friends here when we got lost. Yeah, I like it. And look here, squaw girl, if you don't go along with this plan, we'll just kill you and then take some more hostages, and we may kill a few people just for the hell of it. Their lives are in your hands little lady, so do you think you can play along?" Richard said, pulling the revolver from his pocket and rubbing the gun barrel between Willow's breasts. She nodded, the hate practically seeping from her skin.

"Good girl, I knew you could be a good sport," Richard said, slapping her bottom as he turned away. The men went to work hiding the bags and the long guns under the bushes as Willow stared at the church, the singing still coming from inside. The singing had not stopped—even for a second—since they had first heard it, which could have been longer than half an hour ago by now.

"That's a bad place," Meg said from behind Willow. By

this point Willow wasn't even startled by the girl's appearances, but was simply getting tired of them. She turned to find Meg staring at the church. She didn't take her eyes off of the building, a mixture of disgust and fear on her face. "It's a very bad place," the girl said. Willow surveyed the church again, trying to find something sinister about it, but from its appearance it was just an old church. Of course when she looked back behind her, Meg was gone. Willow contemplated warning the men about the church, but wasn't sure how she would even start.

Moe walked over with Eddie's survival knife, brandishing it wickedly. Willow backed up as he approached her, something in his manner indicating there had been a change in plans and they had decided to just murder her here after all. She was about to turn and run when he spoke.

"Hold your hands up. Come on, we don't have all day," Moe said, indicating he was going to cut her hands free. She lifted her hands up and he roughly cut through the extension cord, the blade easily slicing through the makeshift handcuffs. Willow rubbed her wrists to get some circulation back into them, very relieved to have them free.

Richard walked over to her, "Let me see your wrists." She held her hands up and he inspected them. They were rubbed a little raw and had some reddening, but thankfully the skin wasn't torn and there would be very little bruising. "Okay, that's fine. I didn't want the preacher man to see your wrists all messed up and get a little curious." He turned back to Moe and Bones, "We good to go now?"

Bones nodded, patting his pocket where he had stowed the .50 caliber and an extra clip. Moe nodded too, sliding the survival knife out of sight. Willow knew Richard also had the small revolver. Willow also knew that unless she got lucky and some old lady had a gun in her purse, or some of the men were old time pistol packers, they would still have everyone outgunned. The singing had still not stopped, and the sounds of worship floated through the air as they prepared to approach the church.

"All right, folks, it's show time!" Richard said as he led the group into the churchyard. As they neared, storm clouds had begun to gather. The storm must have been moving in quickly, as they had seen no signs of rain before now. Lightning split the sky and thunder echoed in the distance, causing the group to hurry. Willow was afraid this was a sign.

As they neared the church, they each took time to peek into the windows. The church appeared to be mostly full, although due to its small size a full house was maybe thirty people. There was a pastor up at the podium in the front, and the pews were filled with people of various ages. There were both black and white churchgoers and the ages ranged from the elderly to families with small children. Nothing appeared out of place, so the group came up to the door and Richard knocked lightly. The singing never stopped, so Richard knocked harder. There was still no response, and this close to the church the singing was very loud, so it wasn't surprising they couldn't be heard. Richard knocked again, this time too hard to be polite. When the singing still didn't stop, he shrugged and opened the door, stepping into the church as the others followed.

The four entered the back area of the church and stood silently, giving the congregation time to study them. It was beginning to get very dark in the church as the clouds outside thickened, and as they had surmised there were no electric lights inside. They stood at the back of the church, behind everyone but the pastor, who currently had his eyes closed as he was lost in song.

The four gawked at each other, unsure of exactly what to do. They scanned the congregation. The crowd was mostly older folks, both black and white. There were maybe three families, each with two small children. The children ranged in ages from five to ten and the parents were mostly middle aged. They were all dressed up in their Sunday best with suits and ties and fancy dresses everywhere. It could most likely be attributed to the strange day they had experienced and the pressure of the situation, but none of the four had stopped to think how unusual it was for church to be in session at that time of day and on that day of the week.

Lighting struck again, somewhere nearby this time, and the thunder rolled closer. Richard walked to the front of the church, and as he passed each row, the seated people began to notice him. Each row he passed went silent, and when he was about halfway down the aisle, it had gotten quieter, and before he knew it everyone had stopped singing, including the pastor. The pastor himself was a very tall man, nearly as tall as Bones, but even skinnier. He was bald on top with tufts of gray hair all around the sides of his head. His face was very gaunt, practically skeletal, and his eyes were dark, practically black. No one said a word as the congregation noted the newcomers, turning around to rubberneck at all of them, who were very uncomfortable under the gaze of the group.

Sill no one had spoken, so Richard broke the silence. "I do apologize for interrupting this fine service you folks had going, but my friends and I are in a bit of a pickle, and we wondered if maybe one of you fine Christians could help us out." Richard smiled a smile that would have been at home on a toothpaste box, and Willow wondered how such a handsome man could have such an ugly soul.

The pastor spoke, "Welcome to my church, good sir! I am Pastor Fred Lesheter and this is my flock!" He spread his hands to encompass the entire room as the rest of the congregation remained silent, still staring at the newcomers. Willow noticed a nameplate affixed to the pastor's podium and something about it drew her attention, but the stares of the crowd were oppressive and she didn't have time to ponder it.

"Thank you very much, kind sir. My friends and I, were out camping down in this blasted swamp, and I'm afraid we wandered off and got lost. That's why us city folk need to stick to concrete and street signs, I guess you could say," Richard said, turning the charm on. So far, no one had shown any emotion other than the pastor. The group just stared at them blankly, and if Willow didn't know better, she would swear she saw something sinister in the eyes of the group, from the oldest octogenarians to the youngest children. Something was *wrong* about this church, and she thought back to Meg's warning.

"I'm sure we'd be glad to help you in any way we can, just what can we do for you? And please, just call me Pastor Fred," Pastor Fred said, stepping from behind the podium and smiling broadly at the group, from Richard to the rest of them and then back to Richard.

"We either need a ride of some sort, or if that's not possible, could someone just point us to civilization? Even a gas station would be fine, just something that's not mud and mosquitoes," Richard said, still smiling. At this point it got very dark in the church, like flipping a light switch, and the rain began to pour down, the sound of the water hitting the roof filling the church as it became too dark to even make out faces. Willow didn't like this at all, it was pitch black and you could just barely make out the outlines of the group surrounding them.

Richard backed down the aisle and the four huddled together now at the back of the church, Bones putting his hand on the Desert Eagle as Moe wrapped his hand around the hilt of the knife. Richard had already palmed the small .22 revolver, ready to use it if needed. The group had left the door opened slightly then they entered, and a gust of wind blew it closed, and they heard a slight click after the door slammed. They had been locked in.

They found themselves surrounded by dozens of red dots, as if fireflies had been set loose in the church. The group wondered just what was going on when they realized it wasn't fireflies at all; it was the eyes of the congregation that glowed red in the pitch darkness. The pastor's red eyes glowed brighter as he walked down the aisle towards them.

"Please children, don't be afraid! Let us help you!" Pastor Fred said as he approached the group. Willow backed up until reaching the door behind her and she tugged at it, and sure enough, it was locked tight. Suddenly the church was filled with moans and growls and hisses, as if a pack of wild animals had appeared.

Willow thought back to the nameplate she had seen on the podium and grinned despite herself when she figured out what it had said. *F. Lesheter. F. Lesheter. Flesheter. FLESHEATER!* She giggled wildly as the horror overcame her and she turned back to the church. It was completely black now, the storm raging outside, and the only light inside, the eerie red glow from the monsters' eyes. The men had left the flashlights in the bag since the day had been bright when they had started into the church.

Lighting once again struck, and the bright flashes lit up a scene of Hell inside the church. The members of the congregation were all rotting corpses now, still dressed in their Sunday best. Of course they were—it's what they had all been buried in. The church was a congregation of ghouls. When the lightning flashed, it showed a church full of dead bodies, all in different stages of decomposition, some fairly fresh while others were desiccated to not much more than skeletons. Even worse was the smell. The church had held no particular odor at first, but as soon as the congregation was seen in its true form, the smell of decay filled the air. It was a sickly sweet smell, a combination of an old musty attic with an underlying stench of rot.

The groans and grunts of the ghouls filled the air, but what bothered Willow the most was the loud, piercing scream that threatened to burst her eardrums and grated on her nerves like nails on a chalkboard. It wasn't until her throat began to get sore that she realized the scream was coming from her.

To the men's credit, they didn't let the sight of the monsters freeze them in place. As the ghouls rushed towards them, the loud report of the Desert Eagle echoed in the hall as Bones began to attack. He was hitting the ghouls with head shots, more from habit than anything else, but it so happened decapitation was a method for killing ghouls, and the large exits wounds of the .50 caliber effectively blew the creatures' heads off with each shot. The smaller pops of the .22 were also heard, but sounded very weak when compared to the larger gun. The small handgun was next to useless, but Richard had to try. He put the empty gun back in his pocket without thinking, even knowing it was useless, he felt better having it on his person.

Willow had been huddled against the door, unable to open it no matter how hard she pushed and pulled. Richard shoved her out of the way and gave the door several hard kicks, as well as running into it shoulder first. It didn't budge. They were locked in and weren't getting out through that door.

Richard acted immediately, grabbing Willow and pushing her towards the nearest window. "Bones, clear the way to this window, now!" he ordered, as the rain came down and more thunder and lightning erupted. The ghouls were now nothing more than ravenous beasts, hungry for their next meal. Bones popped in a fresh clip, and even in the poor lightning and chaotic environment managed to kill the ghouls between them and the closest window. The loud gun fired again, a ghoul's head exploding with each shot. Willow was pushed along with Richard behind her, and she wondered if Richard really cared about saving her or was just using her as a human shield. She was pretty sure it was the latter.

As Richard pushed her through the open window, Willow heard Moe scream. They had lost him in the throng. Just before she was pushed outside, she caught a glimpse of him when lightning struck again. He was stabbing and slashing at the ghouls with the large survival knife as a ghoul bit his neck, tearing the flesh away like tissue paper as a fountain of blood erupted from the wound. This served to help the remaining trio, as the hot blood spurting in the midst of the crowd drew the other ghouls to Moe as if they'd heard a dinner bell. She saw Moe get pulled to the ground, a mass of ghouls tearing and biting at him. She saw organs, blood and even white bone as the ghouls ripped him to pieces, his screams lost in the sounds of the satisfied moans of the monsters.

Willow fell out headfirst, landing on the hard ground and seeing stars as she rolled in the deep puddles left by the pouring rain. Richard came out of the window right after her, landing on top of her as he fell to the ground. Bones slid out of the window last, making it about halfway out before he appeared to be stuck. Richard reached up and grabbed one of Bones' arms in both of his, using his full body weight to drag Bones out of the window. All three of them landed in huge mud puddle as lightning struck once again.

Richard grabbed Bones by the shoulder and yelled into his ear, "Get her and get away, now!'

Bones didn't speak but instead grabbed Willow by the waist of her jeans, lifting her easily and carrying her away with one hand. Richard pulled the last grenade from his pocket, yanking out the pin and tossing it into the open window of the church before he ran and made a dive towards the edge of the churchyard.

Lightning flashed again, showing some of the ghouls trying to climb out of the windows to come after them, but there was a loud explosion and all of the glass blew out of the church with a loud crash!

Flames erupted from the church as the dry and desiccated husks of the ghouls went up in flames, burning like they had been doused in gasoline. Within seconds the entire church was burning, the howls of the ghouls echoing in the dark.

Bones kept a tight grip on Willow as the three of them

hurried over to retrieve the bags of guns and money, and then headed down the now muddy and washed out road as fast as they could run. They kept looking back but it appeared as though they weren't being followed. The trio continued down the road, away from the church, until even the flames were no longer visible in the distance. Strangely, once they had gotten about a mile away from the church, the weather cleared up. They were soaked to the bone and covered in mud as they observed blue sky and bright sunshine, and continued on the road to nowhere.

TWELVE

Shade and Waya heard the muffled gunshots, this time coming from the east. The shots weren't as loud but were still clearly audible. They turned and set off in the direction of the gunshots. They couldn't tell whether the shots sounded weak because they were further in the distance, or perhaps there was another reason. In this godforsaken swamp, any explanation could be possible.

Soon they heard a loud thump, and were rewarded not long after by a smoke trail overhead. They grinned, having a clear cut destination for a change. Neither man allowed himself to think of Willow being in the midst of the gunfire, at this point they were just operating under the assumption she was safe and they would soon rescue her.

The land eventually became firmer and less spongy, and they were grateful for firm ground to walk on for a change. Shade followed right on Waya's footsteps and soon bumped right into his back as he stopped abruptly. Shade raised his gun, wondering what had spooked Waya. Waya held his hand up to indicate silence, and soon the ground began to shake ever so slightly. He stayed very still, sweat beading on his forehead as the trembling became more pronounced.

Shade heard the trees and bushes rustling in the distance as if a big wind was blowing through, but he knew this was no wind. *Something* was in the woods with them, and it was something big. The sound of the limbs snapping and bushes bending grew louder and louder, and the entire ground began to quake as whatever it was passed by them. Both men strained their eyes to try to determine just what could possibly be causing this type of disturbance, but nothing appeared to them. Eventually the sound began to fade.

The two stood in place quietly until they could no longer

hear the trees snapping or feel the ground shake. They exchanged worried glances. They both knew they had just dodged a bullet, and were really happy they never laid eyes on whatever the hell that was that had just passed near them. After waiting a few minutes just to be sure, the two continued on their way.

The smoke was black and still coming up in the distance, but it appeared to already be weakening since it had first come to their attention. Thankfully it didn't appear to be too far away, and the men were confident they would be able to find the source of the fire now even if it did burn out. The men were walking through thick forest when they reached a clearing. The clearing came out of nowhere, as was common for this swamp. The two had stumbled into open ground before they realized it, and they were two seasoned outdoorsmen. They both stood still for a second and took in their surroundings.

Even though it was unlikely, the two had come upon some sort of structure in the middle of the swamp, what appeared to be a mausoleum. It was small and appeared to be made of marble, Greek columns adorning the stone stairs leading up to the doorway. There were also numerous statues all over the clearing, too many to count. The men stared in wonder at the numerous stone sculptures scattered all over the clearing, which was covered in thick green vegetation. The figures appeared to have been there a while, as several of them were covered in vines, but for some reason the stone itself appeared to have no wear. The statues were exposed to the elements, but showed no trace of the weathering such exposure would cause.

"I think we better switch our handguns to silver, just in case," Waya cautioned, and both men swapped out their clips for bullets loaded with silver.

The two moved in cautiously to get a better look at the various effigies. Probably even more unusual than the strange positioning of the many statues, were the unusual sculptures themselves. Some were warriors from various time periods but once again they were not arranged in any particular order. Native American Warriors stood side by side with Civil War Soldiers. Revolutionary War Soldiers stood beside what appeared to be simple hunters. There were also several modern statues, random things such as fisherman, campers and even children, several of them in modern dress. What was most disturbing about the sculptures were the horrified expressions on the faces of each, as if the sculptor had attempted to catch each subject in the midst of the most terrifying moment imaginable.

One of the statues even resembled a game warden, and Waya walked over for a closer inspection. He took a deep breath, and Shade walked over beside him wondering what he had found.

"This statue looks just like Stevie Brenneman. He was training to be a game warden here and disappeared back in '84. Why the hell would a statue of him be out here? And see here, they got it right even down to his name tag," Waya said, tapping the stone tag with a fingertip.

A horrible thought hit Shade, and he surveyed the myriad statues. "No way, you have got to be shitting me..." he said before the doors of the mausoleum burst open and the sound of the largest rattlesnake in history buzzed through the air.

Shade turned his back to the building and covered Waya's eyes with his palm, tackling him to the ground. "Get down and don't look at it!" he said as an arrow flew through the air, smacking against the statue and shattering. The men examined the shards of the arrow, noticing it was covered in a thick black ichor with a sickening smell.

"I don't believe this. Don't look at her, it's a damn gorgon," Shade said, dragging Waya to his feet and pulling him into the woods, both of them dragging their heavy bags along with them.

Another arrow sliced through the woods, missing both men as they stumbled through them. The two halted before they plunged right into the black waters of the swamp. Water now surrounded them. Even though the two men had walked into the clearing, they now found themselves on an island.

"Oh, this day just keeps getting better," Shade said, walking along the edge of the bank but finding no land anywhere. The small clearing was now completely enclosed by the dark water of the hellish swamp. The hissing of the monster and the sound of the rattles filled the air as Waya and Shade hurried along the back, keeping the trees between themselves and the gorgon as they heard arrows being fired into the thickets.

"A gorgon? You mean Medusa? Turn you to stone with her gaze and all that shit? Damn, why would I even be surprised..." Waya said, causing Shade to cock his head.

"Okay so the bitch is shooting poison arrows at us, she's basically a giant snake who can bite us and kill us, and we can't even look at her without turning into one of those ugly statues. That about cover it?" Waya said.

"Yeah, I think you got it. I think the only way to kill her is to cut her head off, but first we have to figure out a way to watch her. I think you can look at her reflection, just not right at her. You got a mirror on you?" Shade asked hopefully.

Waya was straight-faced. "No, I left my compact back on the boat."

"Shit, what can we...wait, I got it!" Shade said, reaching into his pocket and pulling out his sunglasses case. He opened it up and pulled out his mirrored lenses. "Ha! And people tried to tell me the 80's called and wanted these back!"

Shade held them up and tried to see behind him, barely able to do so. "This isn't going to work too well, but I guess we don't have a choice."

An arrow thudded into the tree right near Shade's head, and the two grabbed their bags and hurried back the way they had came, being sure to stay right at the waterline to keep the trees and bushes between them and the monster. The two were also uneasy about being this near the water, but they really had no choice.

Waya pulled out his machete and Shade thought a second. "You know, a grenade will blow that bitch's head off just like a blade can cut it off, let me try that first."

"You do it your way, and I'll do it mine," Waya said as he wrapped his bandanna around his eyes tightly and sat down Indian style on the ground, beginning to quietly chant in a language Shade didn't understand. Shade wasn't sure how to react, so he stepped away from Waya so as not to attract the gorgon to him.

Shade made his way to the opposite side of the clearing, using the trees for cover before he was able to use the glasses to spot the monster. It was even more horrible than he had imagined. She was huge, twenty feet from the top of her head to the huge rattle on her tail, her body about ten feet tall from the waist to ground, which was how she slithered—upright from the "waist" up, if that was the right terminology for such a beast. The bottom half of the body was indeed a rattlesnake, right down to the diamond pattern on the skin, and while the top half did appear to be humanoid, to call her half human would have been inaccurate. The torso was also snake-like but did have human arms attached to it, which were now brandishing the bow and an arrow. There was a quiver attached to the gorgon's back, and it appeared to have no shortage of arrows. The face was the worst part. Even in the reflection, the eyes had a bright glow, and the creature did indeed have snakes for hair, but the face itself was not a woman's but rather just the face of a reptile. It was so alien, it was hard for his mind to process, but everything about the creature repulsed him.

Shade aimed the grenade launcher over his shoulder awkwardly and fired, the grenade missing the gorgon and instead shattering a statue near her in a ball of flame. As shards of marble rained upon the gorgon, she fired an arrow at Shade, tracking him by the direction his grenade had come from and barely missing him. She drew another arrow and slithered towards Shade with impossible speed considering the creature's massive girth. Shade barely had time to pop another grenade in the launcher before she was upon him.

Shade fired again, and this time the grenade was a direct hit, striking the gorgon right in the chest and blowing into the ground in a mass of flame. The trees between him and the monster had protected Shade from most of the blast, but he was still singed. He looked in the glasses as the monster lay prone, and was dismayed as it slowly raised itself back up. The grenade hadn't done much harm to the monster, and it hissed its anger in Shade's direction.

Shade watched as Waya rushed into the clearing behind the gorgon, still blindfolded and with the machete in hand. He took a mighty swing and managed to catch the monster right in the side of the neck from behind, the sharp blade biting deep as thick black blood erupted from the cut, steaming as it hit the air. Waya hacked at the creature's neck as it flopped around helplessly, before he managed to completely sever the beast's head. Shade watched it all happen from the reflection of his glasses, amazed.

Waya stopped and kicked around, searching for the head. "Shade, don't come out yet and don't look this way! The head still has power. Let me take care of it!" Waya shouted, knowing Shade was watching from somewhere hidden. Waya stomped his foot around, stepping right on the head as the snakes it had for hair writhed. The large body was also still slithering and flopping around, the same way any snake would do once its head was removed. Shade was a little concerned the large corpse might bump into Waya, but so far it hadn't come close. Waya held the head down with his foot as he chopped at the soft earth near it with the machete. The black ichor was still spurting from the corpse and smoking, and everywhere the sticky substance dripped the grass turned brown and died.

"Watch out for that damn body flopping around, it's spewing that nasty blood out and it's acid," Shade called out, still watching from his mirrored lenses.

"Yeah, it stinks like shit. I think I can avoid it by smell alone," Waya called back, as he chopped a hole in the ground. He leaned over and stuck the machete into the hole, trying to judge its depth. He chopped a little more, digging out some of the rich soil with the blade before checking it again. He repeated the process several times before he was satisfied with the hole he had dug, and then he rolled the head into the hole and began to push the soil back over it. Shade watched until the head was completely underground and then came out of his hiding place, carrying his bag along with him.

"It's safe now. The body's not a danger right?" Shade questioned as he made his way to Waya, who was tamping the soil down tighter over the skull in the dirt.

Waya removed the bandana and wiped his forehead with it before wrapping it around his forehead once again. "Right, just the eyes have the power from what I understand. Jesus, that thing stinks too," Waya said, holding his nose.

Shade sniffed. "I don't think it's just the body or blood. A terrible smell is coming out of that damn sepulcher," Shade said, stepping over to the stairs and peeking into the opening but only seeing pitch black. He opened his bag and took out a flashlight, shining it into the gloom but still unable to see a thing. "You don't think there's another one of these things down there do you?"

Waya shook his head, "If there was I think we'd know it by now. Let me get my bag and we'll try to figure a way off of this island."

Waya walked back to get his bag near the bank as Shade tried unsuccessfully to see what was in the mausoleum. A terrible stench wafted from inside, an overwhelming scent of rotting meat.

"Hey Shade, come here a minute," Waya called from just the other side of the trees. Shade walked over and was stunned to see they were no longer on an island. Just like magic, land had filled in the black water they had spotted earlier.

"Man, I hate this place," Shade muttered before the two of them walked back into the center of the clearing.

"Let's clean this up. I'm going to toss a grenade on this body, why don't you drop one down in that damn hole there and let's get back to finding my daughter." Waya said, removing one of the grenades from his bag. Shade walked up the stairs, pumping his grenade launcher before firing into the black abyss. There was a muffled explosion from deep within the sepulcher, but very little flame washed from the doorway. There was a deep tunnel inside the building, and no telling what had awaited them inside.

As they walked off, each of them carrying their weapons and their bags, Waya tossed a grenade onto the body, igniting it as it thrashed about. The smoke trail had stopped by this point, but both men knew the general direction by now as they headed that way, leaving the unholy garden of stone death behind them to burn.

THIRTEEN

THE CIVIL WAR ERA

The rebel forces had been in retreat ever since the fort fell, the Yankees washing over the walls of the fort like the banks of river overflowing during a flood. The small company of men was barely able to escape, but escape they had, even managing to bring along a few cannons. Colonel Hubert E. Dillard had managed to lead about thirty men and three cannons out of the jaws of the Yankee death trap and deep into the swamps of good old Georgia herself. The Colonel wasn't sure exactly what his next step would be once the men got away, but they had all been so happy not to have been killed or captured, no one was questioning the quality of his leadership.

None of the group had managed to get away with any horses, and even the cannons were being dragged along solely by manpower, but they had all their muskets and pistols, and a good supply of ammo, including cannonballs and gunpowder. If only there was some way this small group of men could retake the fort, then the name of Hubert E. Dillard would definitely go down in history as a true god among men!

At this point however, Colonel Dillard was simply lost. He wasn't even sure where this damned swamp had come from, although with the fort sitting on the edge of the water, naturally marsh land would be nearby. Still, he had explored all of the areas near the fort before, and had never come upon this swamp. There had been a mad scramble to retreat when the blues first attacked, so it was possible they all got turned around and ended up in unfamiliar territory. The Colonel hoped one of the men would speak up if they knew where they were, because his pride wouldn't allow him to admit he was lost.

The group rolled into a small clearing, the ground soft but not as soft as it had been in places. The group had come through some areas of mud so thick it was akin to quicksand, and they nearly lost the cannon in the mire, but the men all worked together and managed to save all three of them. The cannon could be the difference between life and death for these men, so they had all worked hard to preserve them.

As they all shuffled into the clearing, the Colonel called a halt to the procession, wanting to give the men time to rest and gather themselves. "Halt! Everyone at ease, I think we are all due for a little rest now," Colonel Dillard said, himself taking a seat right on the grass and leaning his back against a nearby oak tree. The other men followed suit, especially the men who had been charged with dragging the cannon along. Several of them laid flat on their backs in the soft grass and were snoring within a few minutes.

The Colonel allowed the men whatever form of relaxation they desired. He knew the Yankees were more concerned with the capture of the fort rather than the pursuit of a few soldiers, so he didn't feel as though they were under great pressure. The mosquitoes and humidity were terrible, but the men were also exhausted, and the layers of sweat and grime covering their skin acted as a partial bug repellant, and before long the entire group was napping.

A loud roar awoke the Colonel, who snapped his head up, wondering what could possibly have made the sound he heard. He listened but heard nothing. He saw most of the men were still snoring, but there were a few who were looking around with the same expression he had, like they had heard something but weren't sure if it was real or imagined.

The ground began to tremble. Slightly, but it was there. Then the ground began to quake, and it was unmistakable this time—something was out there. From the feel of it, it had to be thousands of Yankee soldiers, as no smaller amount could make the very ground quake as it was doing now.

"Wake up! Wake up you lazy bastards and man those cannons! Load 'em up and get 'em ready, it's time for battle!" Colonel Dillard ordered, drawing his saber and waving it around for emphasis.

As the men all readied the cannons and their guns, not

quite sure where to aim but trying to ready themselves nonetheless, another loud roar split the air. It was the most frightening sound any of the men had ever heard, and these were hardened southerners who had no fear of the howl of wolves or the screech of the wildcat. This was something different. What war machine had the dreaded North invented to unleash upon them now?

Then, the men saw it. Even taller than the trees, the head of the Tyrannosaurus Rex came into view, huge and wide, its head a cross between a snake and an alligator. None of the men had any idea what a T-Rex was, but when it tore through the trees and into the clearing it was as though the devil himself had appeared to drag them all to Hell.

The T-Rex roared again as it watched the men scurry around the field, his beady eyes following them before he leaned down and plucked the nearest man up, tossing him back and swallowing him in one gulp. He roared again, this time a roar of pleasure, expressing how much he enjoyed the taste of the human flesh he had just consumed. He leaned his great head down once more—the man he had targeted attempting to flee but finding it futile—and its jaws closed, bisecting him. The T-Rex chewed his food better this time, munching the man between his huge teeth before swallowing him down as well.

Once again the T-Rex roared, very pleased to have found such a great food source in one place. He began to stalk the battlefield, squishing some of the men underfoot but still leaning down to eat from time to time.

Until this point, the men had all been paralyzed with fear while facing this demon from Hell, but now, after seeing the carnage the creature had wrought, fear was being replaced with anger. These men were all veterans of the bloodiest battles in history, and whether the enemy was a soldier wearing navy blue or a giant lizard, they were prepared to bring it down.

The men began to fire at the dinosaur, taking careful aim with their muskets and letting fly. Then they would draw their revolvers, firing at the beast until their cylinders were emptied. It was all to no avail, the small lead balls couldn't penetrate the thick hide of the prehistoric beast. Still they tried, the men going down fighting as the monster stomped and ground them up with his teeth.

By this point, Colonel Dillard had regained his senses and had come to terms with the fact he was facing a monster. Now it was time to do something about it.

"You men, rally that cannon! Load it up and let's give this big son of a bitch a taste of good southern iron!" Colonel Dillard said, the men following his orders and loading the cannon. The beast had already stomped one of the cannons to pieces on its initial charge into the clearing, and the men watched helplessly as it swung its great tail, sending men flying and destroying the other cannon. They only had one cannon left, and they aimed to let that bastard know it.

"Fire at will! Kill that damned beast from Hell!" Colonel Dillard said, still holding his saber in hand and waving it at the monster in defiance.

The men loaded the cannon and fired, the huge ball sailing through the air and striking the dinosaur right in the torso, the cannon ball ripping into the creature's abdomen and blowing a large hole in its midsection.

The dinosaur stopped its rampage for a second and looked down at the hole, wondering how this was possible. The men used this lull to reload the cannon and fire again. This time the ball hit the T-Rex a little higher, catching it in the chest and blowing one of its forearms to shreds. The great beast staggered back and roared in pain and in anger. *How dare my food fight back? Do they not understand they exist only to feed me?*

The T-Rex was badly wounded, but now it spotted the cannon as the men worked feverishly to reload. It roared and charged. The men were torn between fleeing and trying to ready the cannon, and the creature was so close they decided to go with reloading since they wouldn't have time to run very far. The beast was upon them, its great jaws wide open to swallow them and the cannon whole. Colonel Dillard was off to the side and winced as he watched the men and cannon about to disappear into the beast's maw. At the last second the cannon fired, and this time the cannonball went right down the monster's gullet and exploded in its throat, blowing the monster's head clean off as the men scattered and the huge monster fell onto the cannon, dead.

The monster had managed to destroy the cannon with its last act, but it was finished at this point. The remaining men cheered as the creature jerked in its death throes.

Colonel Dillard surveyed the carnage on the battlefield. It was as bad as anything he had seen in this cursed war of necessity. Bodies were everywhere, although in most cases it was pieces of bodies. He did a quick head count and saw ten men. Over two thirds of their meager force had been wiped out in minutes by this spawn of the Devil. He supposed a few men could have managed to flee into the swamp, but he doubted they would return. Nothing could scare a man more than fear of the unknown, and this great demon was definitely unknown.

The Colonel was contemplating his next action when he heard a strange chirping, like a bird, but it was not a bird call the Colonel recognized. Colonel Dillard then felt something tug on his coat, and found himself face to face with another giant lizard.

This one was much smaller than the giant Tyrannosaurus, not much bigger than a man. Colonel Dillard found himself staring at this dinosaur eye to eye, and the lizard just stared back with a quizzical expression. The Colonel had no way of knowing it, but he was face to face with a velociraptor. It didn't appear to mean him harm, but instead just studied him, chirping in childlike fashion.

The Colonel smiled at the lizard, wondering if perhaps this would be a much gentler creature than the large one had been. The dinosaur was eyeing the Colonel's stomach, so the Colonel followed its gaze to see what had interested the creature.

He gazed down and beheld his intestines hanging from his body. He looked back at the lizard and saw the large hooked claws on its forearms, and realized the slight tug he had felt earlier had been this thing disemboweling him. He surmised from the blood and guts dripping down his pants that he would soon be dead. He had been so excited and filled with adrenaline he hadn't even noticed.

He was hearing screams, screams which had been in the back of his mind all along but which he hadn't paid much attention to. He watched as the remainder of his men was eaten alive by scores of lizards just like the one facing him now. A few of the men attempted to fight, shooting at the monsters with their muskets, stabbing them with their bayonets, peppering them with the revolvers, and even slashing at them with their swords. A few of the lizards were even killed, but it was all hopeless. The lizards were too fast and too hardy. The men were only delaying the inevitable. Colonel Dillard gawked at lizard that was still only a few feet away from him. The lizard chirped again, and then pounced on him, tackling him to the ground as it started to feed.

FOURTEEN

The trio was very cautious after the incident at the church. What had started as a four way split had now turned into halves, but at this point either man would have gladly given up his share of the cash in order to find a nice hotel and a good restaurant, and be out of this damned shit-hole of a swamp.

Willow was still being dragged along, still not finding the right opportunity to escape, and also wondering if at this point she would be better off on her own or with the two men. She had always heard talk of a haunted swamp in the area, but her father had always told her to put no stock in such tales, and always changed the subject whenever it was brought up. Willow was beginning to see her father had known about this place the entire time, and had only been trying to protect her. Normally she would feel pissed off about him trying to shelter her—a grown woman—but after seeing this place, she was damn glad he had sheltered her from it, and she wished she could have stayed sheltered from it forever. The men had heard explosions earlier, but neither could agree on exactly what it would have been. They could think of no reason anyone pursuing them would have explosives, so they had written it off as coincidence. Perhaps someone was out in the swamp trying to blow up stumps or something equally mundane.

The three still had no idea where they were at, or where they were headed, and it was getting late in the day. In just a few hours it would be dark, and they didn't relish the idea of being out here after nightfall. Richard had already been scoping out locations to make a camp, deciding they may be better off preparing for the night now so they could make a defensible position, rather than waiting until after dark and having to deal with who knows what at the same time they tried to set up some type of shelter. The problem being, Richard had found nothing suitable. This place was just damn inhospitable.

The three were all moving along a thickly wooded trail, lost in their own thoughts, when they came upon a chain-link fence. They halted, staring at the fence like they had never seen one. The fence wasn't new, but didn't appear to be very old either. They traveled along the fence and once again found themselves shocked. It was a trailer park.

There was a good, old fashioned, tornado magnet trailer park right out here in the middle of the damned swamp. Richard hopped the fence, and Bones picked Willow up and lifted her over like a small child before he simply stepped over the fence. The three of them walked cautiously into the park, the two men keeping their guns at the ready.

So far no one was visible, but the trailers did appear inhabited. It was a fairly small park, maybe ten trailers on two acres. The trailers were all small single-wides, and a couple were even travel trailers with the wheels removed. It was packed pretty tightly, but the trailers were all small enough to fit. There was even electricity in the park, as a few of the trailers had their porch lights on even though it wasn't near dark yet.

"I'll be damned. We found civilization! And fancy too! That damn trailer over there is bricked in! With real red bricks! Whoo, we made it pardner!" Richard said, slapping Bones on the shoulder. Bones grinned slightly but from his expression he still wasn't convinced.

"You thought you'd made it at the church too, and you saw how that turned out," Willow said, the ordeal of the day loosening her tongue.

"Oh come on now, that was a church. Everybody knows those places are evil. This is a goddamned Georgia trailer park! Who the hell's gonna haunt a trailer park, the ghost of Rhoda the meth whore and Billy the pig poker? Come on, this is just good old redneck livin' here. There ain't nothing bad here! Other than maybe herpes, but we ain't here to play!" Richard said, grinning and happy. He scrutinized the area. "Shit, I don't see a goddamned car anywhere in this bitch. This is ridiculous, doesn't anybody drive anymore? Man, I've been in some rough trailer parks in my time, but never one where nobody could afford a car!"

The trio walked through the park, still seeing no signs of

life, but it did feel as though they were being watched. "Now, this time we won't bother hiding the guns, I don't think anyone in here will bat an eye at them anyway. We were out on a hunting trip and got lost, got it?" Richard said to Bones, who nodded and then looked at Willow.

"Hunting with a machine gun and a combat shotgun?" Willow said sarcastically.

"Honey, people hunt with these types of guns all the time down south, if anything they'll think this is a semi-auto AR-15. Trust me, we're good. And as long as they don't get a peek at the money in our bags we won't even have to explain anything," Richard said.

"What if they saw the robbery on the news? I'm sure it's all over the place by now," Willow said, feeling very argumentative for some reason, even if it was in her best interest to stay quiet.

"Damn, I hadn't thought of that. In that case, we'd just have to shoot 'em," Richard said with a shrug.

Willow shook her head as she realized he wasn't joking in the slightest. The three continued to walk around the park, trying to find a person somewhere. "Hey Bones, how are we doing on ammo?" Richard asked as he unzipped his bag and counted his remaining clips. He still had three full clips of thirty rounds, and a full clip in the gun.

"I got a clip in the Eagle, and one more in the bag, and I dunno how many shotgun shells, there's still twenty or so maybe," Bones said, opening up the bag and checking.

Richard nodded, satisfied that they still had enough bullets to get themselves out of a jam if it came to that. Willow was still wondering how to play this, as whatever happened in this trailer park could determine whether she lived or died. The three walked by one of the trailers, the biggest one in the lot, and heard the doorknob rattle as the door opened. Both men aimed their guns slightly in the direction of the door, ready to open fire if needed.

Instead the door opened and a young girl stood in the doorway, head cocked to the side and her legs crossed as she peered out at them. It was hard to judge her age—she could have been anywhere from fourteen to twenty-one as her body had begun to develop—but she still appeared young in the face. She wore a tight, white t-shirt, mostly see-through, and it was obvious she wasn't wearing a bra to cover her ample chest. She was also wearing cut-off jeans shorts, cut way too high as the bottom of her ass cheeks were hanging out. She was the epitome of a trailer park Lolita, an underage sexpot that was always out for trouble, and was so sexy she usually found it. Her long blonde hair was stringy and out of place and her blue eyes sparkled. If she was in a better environment, she might have even made it as a model, although she was too short for that as she was five feet tall at best.

"Hey ya'll, what's up?" she said in a slow, southern drawl.

Richard grinned at her. She came across so cliché he wondered if someone was playing a joke. "Hello little lady, how are you? My name's Richard, this here's Willow, and the tall fella there, we just call him Bones."

The girl examined Richard over, barely acknowledged Willow, and then stared at Bones. Bones grinned at her and she smiled back. Richard was taken aback at this, as usually women swooned all over him, and this hot little filly was more interested in Bones. He guessed she was maybe attracted to the danger, as there was something scary about Bones and this girl might never have been out of the trailer park, so danger had to be attractive. Bones licked his lips at the girl. He always had liked them young.

"Hey, I'm Carol," the girl said, speaking directly to Bones now. "What brings you to this fine getaway of ours?"

"Carol, who the hell are you talking to, you little whore? If it's one of them Oakley boys again I'm gonna tan your ass!" A voice yelled from inside the trailer, and a woman appeared behind Carol in the doorway. The three were taken aback, as the woman looked so much like what had to be her daughter, it was hard to process.

The woman was taller than Carol, and maybe twenty years older, and she showed every bit of those twenty years. She was still attractive, but she had this worn look about her. Her hair was just like her daughter's, but thinner and with split ends. She was dressed the same, although her t-shirt was black and not as tight, and her cut-offs weren't as short. They were both barefoot, and both had gold ankle bracelets. She was skinnier than Carol. The bottom line being whereas Carol was too hot for the trailer park, her mother was the poster girl for 'trailer-park-hot'.

"Oh, I'm sorry, I didn't know we had company," the mother said, running her fingers through her hair as a makeshift comb. "I'm Malinda, and I guess you've already met Carol." Malinda regarded Carol with disdain and Carol returned the look without turning to face her.

"We are sorry to intrude, ladies, but we were out hunting and we got lost in this damn swamp, and we were wondering if perhaps you two could point us in the direction of the nearest town." Richard said, checking both of the women out. He didn't think either of them was as hot as Willow, but there was nothing that said he couldn't play the field a little. Then again, these two in the trailer were too eager for his tastes. He preferred it when they fought and scratched, but not to get him *into* bed, which appeared be the case with these two trailer park hotties.

"The nearest town is just a shortcut through them woods right over there, but why don't you all come in and get something to drink? I don't mean to offend, but you all look like you've been through hell today!" Malinda said, taking Carol by the shoulders and moving her from the doorway as she waved the trio in.

Carol whispered just loud enough to be overheard, "Mom, why don't you just wear a damn mattress on your back and stop playing coy?"

"You shut up and show some class!" Malinda said, also just loud enough to be overheard.

Willow still wasn't sure how best to play this. She didn't want to get the two women raped and killed (and not necessarily in that order), so she had to play things cool. She decided she'd wait for her chance and either warn them, or just try to make a break for it and hope for the best. Things were getting down to the wire now, and she might have to make some hard choices about her survival versus other people's. She also found to her dismay that Richard had been right about the guns. The two women had not given the weapons a second glance and had taken the hunting story for truth right away.

Richard and Bones shrugged at one another as the two women walked back into the trailer, wondering what they should do next. If the two women had seen the story on the news they could have already dialed 911 and might just be stalling them until the cops showed up. The one thing that could give them away would be Willow, whose picture might have been shown on the news. Richard cursed mentally at the thought and knew they should have killed her and dumped her body before coming into the trailer park. There would always be other fish in the sea. Regardless, this wasn't the time for second guessing.

Richard shrugged and walked into the trailer, the rickety steps leading into the door rocking under his weight as there was no porch. He examined the trailer as he entered, and he knew Bones would be watching out behind them. Bones made sure Willow walked into the trailer behind Richard as they filed inside.

The door led into the living room, and the trailer was actually nice inside. There was a large flat-screen TV as well as a couch and two recliners. The walls were wood panel but high quality, and the carpet was a plush gray, much thicker than one would expect in a mobile home. Richard wondered if the home had been customized, and found himself impressed. Maybe when this was all over he'd put a similar mobile home by a pond somewhere and retire.

Carol grabbed Bones by the hand and pulled him over to the couch, sitting down and indicating he should sit beside her. She stretched out her short but shapely and tanned legs and put her feet on the coffee table, obviously showing off.

Richard caught disdain on Malinda's face at the slutty display her daughter made, before she took a seat in one of the recliners and indicated Richard should sit in the other. Willow sat on the end of the couch beside Bones, taking the one other free seat in the living room.

"Why, you boys do have some big guns, I bet you were going after some big game huh? And what's in those bags?" Malinda said as she sat back in the chair.

"We always use big guns. If we are going to hunt, hunt big I always say. And the bags just have some hunting gear and ammo in them, nothing too important." Richard said, trying to cut off her curiosity

Malinda saw Willow on the couch, acknowledging her for the first time. "Oh, hello there, ma'am, I'm sorry if I was rude! I heard them talking to Carol earlier, so you are Willow? And how are you related to this fine gentleman?" Malinda asked, trying to see how Willow fit into the picture before she moved in for the kill.

"She's my sister, and Bones is our cousin," Richard said before Willow could answer, realizing he should have planned this a little better and went over the rules again before they walked into the trailer park.

Malinda perked up when she found out they were related to Willow, glad to know she wasn't a wife or girlfriend. "Oh, and she's your hunting buddy, huh? No gun for you Willow?" Malinda said, trying to be nice but coming across very fake.

"No, they don't let me carry one, they just let me shoot theirs from time to time," Willow said, smiling her own fake smile right back at Malinda.

Carol and Bones had just been sitting on the couch in silence and staring into each other's eyes all this time, with Carol running her hands up and down Bone's arm as Bones rubbed Carol's knee with his large hand. Even Richard was taken aback at this, and he didn't want Bones getting too aggressive and blowing this whole deal. As far as they knew, the trailer park was full of people and they wanted to draw as little attention as possible.

"Oh, I swear I'd forget my head if it wasn't attached! I promised you all something to drink, didn't I? Carol, get these fine folks some lemonade!" Malinda said, still talking to Richard. When there was no movement from Carol's side of the room, Malinda turned to her and saw her underage daughter and Bones pawing at one another. "Carol! Get these folks some lemonade!" Malinda yelled, slapping Carol on her bare thigh.

"Ow! Okay! DammitT!" Carol said, standing up and walking into the kitchen behind the living room. Everyone was quiet as they heard the rattle of glasses and ice, and a few minutes later Carol came out with three lemonades on a tray. Richard, Bones and Willow all took a glass, and once their hands wrapped around the ice cold beverage they began to suck it down. They hadn't known how thirsty they were until the possibility of an actual drink presented itself, and before they knew it, they'd drained their glasses.

Malinda watched wide-eyed as they drank the liquid down. "My, you three sure were parched! Didn't you bring any water along?"

Richard coughed, the cool drink tightening his dry throat, "We had some, but drank it all earlier before we got lost. We never dreamed we'd be out this long." Richard stared outside. The sun was setting. For some reason both his and Bones watches had stopped working right after the wreck. He assumed they had been damaged then. Willow hadn't been wearing one, so they had had no way to tell time since they had gotten lost in the swamp.

The door to the trailer swung open, and a skinny man wearing a baseball cap, a tank top, torn-up blue jeans and old work boots walked inside. He had long red hair, cut in a mullet and a huge handlebar mustache.

"Damn it Malinda, I told you about keeping this door locked, Carol will have everyone one of them damn Oakley boys in here if we don't—" he stopped talking when he saw the guests in the living room.

"Oh, I'm sorry. I didn't know we had company! Hey there gents, and lady! I'm Red, Malinda's husband and Carol's father. It's nice to see you all!" The man didn't seem at all perturbed to see strange people in his home carrying guns. Malinda didn't even stop staring at Richard, and while Bones did take his hand off of Carol's knee, she continued to rub her hands all over his body as if her father weren't a few feet away.

By this point, Red was interested in Willow, and he was giving her the same kind of looks the women had been giving Richard and Bones. He stared openly for a full minute as Willow ignored him, her disgust more than matching his lust. Red walked over and gave Malinda a kiss, a much more intimate one than would be expected in the company of strangers. Then to make things even stranger, Red leaned over and gave Carol a kiss too—not a French kiss like he had given his wife, but still a kiss on the lips. Carol winked over at Bones during the kiss, but even the stone-cold killer was shocked. He gave Richard a look that said *what the hell have we stumbled into here?* Richard gave him the same look in return, and Willow was ready to bolt from the room and damn the consequences.

Red walked over and stood between the two recliners. Richard spoke, "Oh, I'm sorry. Am I in your seat?" he said, starting to stand.

Red put his hand on his shoulder, stopping him. "No, its fine, I don't mind standing."

A thought occurred to Richard. "So Red, what kind of car

do you drive?" he asked, finally seeing a way to get the hell out of this redneck soap opera.

"Oh I don't drive, I lost my license a while back, DUI and all, so I mostly just walk everywhere," Red said with a grin.

Richard tried to hide his disappointment as he had once again run into a dead end. Red saw the guns the two men had brought in, Bones' shotgun on the coffee table and Richard's rifle on the floor near his chair. The bags were under the guns.

"Oh, you guys were doing some hunting, I see?" Red said, admiring the firearms.

"What an idiot, like anyone hunts with guns like those," Willow said under her breath.

Red heard her mumble but couldn't make out what she said. "I'm sorry miss, did you say something? By the way, what is your name?"

Malinda clapped her hands, "Oh, how rude of me! Red, this is Richard. That tall fella there is Bones, and the girls name is, um, hon, what did you say your name was again?"

"It's Willow," Willow said flatly.

"Pleased to meet you, Willow," Red said, giving her a grin that proudly displayed his tobacco-stained teeth.

Red did a headcount. "What do you know, three girls and three boys, we could have a swing party if we were that type of people, now couldn't we?" Red said, only half laughing and looking around the room with a look that indicated they were indeed that type of people, even if one of the women was his teenage daughter.

At this point, Willow saw that the shotgun wasn't too far from her, and she was ready to snatch it up and begin shooting at everyone in the room, hopefully killing Red first. Red then saw the empty glasses, now filled with melting ice, and for some reason his shoulders drooped. "Oh, y'all had some lemonade I see."

Richard wondered why Red was dejected to know they had lemonade, and he was about to inquire but his tongue was thick—too thick for his mouth. He tried to speak but for some reason he couldn't and his mouth felt stuffed with cotton. He saw Bones and Willow on the couch, but then his vision began to cloud, black closing in on everything he could see. Willow and Bones appeared to be asleep. *What the hell are they doing sleeping at a time like this?*

His vision went black but he could still hear, although everything sounded tinny, as if it were coming from a great distance. Red and Malinda appeared to be arguing, and he could hear loud voices but the words were muddied, sounding underwater. Richard was getting snatches of conversation as he floated further and further from reality.

"Why'd you give it to 'em so fast? I wasn't even home yet!" Red yelled, sounding very exasperated.

"I didn't want to let them get away. It's been a long time since we had company!" Malinda answered defensively.

"Yeah, damn right it has, and when was the last time you saw something as fine as that little Indian gal come into this park? Like, never! I would like to have had a little fun with her!" Red argued.

"You still can!"

"It's no fun when she's like this!"

"Like she'd have had anything to do with you otherwise! You are one dumb sumbitch!"

"Shut up and help me, who goes first?"

Richard faded out.

Shade and Waya had come upon the ruins of the burning church, the smoldering ruins leaving just soot in the air they were able to find it. The graveyard was still visible, and part of the steeple remained unburned, but otherwise there was nothing in the ashes to indicate that it had been a church. The two did quick search of the ashes, and the only thing human they turned up was a badly burnt skeleton that was in several pieces.

"What the hell do you think happened here? Is this a church? You know anything about this place?" Shade asked as he kicked around through the blackened wood.

"It looks like a church, and a graveyard, but what the hell it's doing out here I don't know. Like I told you before, I have heard stories of different kinds of buildings turning up out here from time to time, and churches have been mentioned, but this is the first time I've seen anything like this. What the hell would a church be doing out here anyway? It's in the middle of damn nowhere and you can barely get to the place. I think this is some of that weird shit the swamp brings up." Waya said.

"That skeleton, I guess you know it's too big to be Willow. I mean, I'm no expert, and something has done a number on it, but I have seen some skeletons in my time. It's not her," Shade said, trying to reassure Waya.

"It ain't her, the damn thing had gold fillings or something, and she never had anything like that," Waya answered.

"Damn! I never even thought to check the teeth. This swamp is really getting to me."

"It's getting to both of us. And it's getting late. We only have a few more hours of daylight, if that. I didn't want us to be out after dark."

Shade paused a minute before responding. "Do you want us to head back?"

Waya shook his head. "No, but if you want to I'll lead us out. You've already done more than a lot of men would, so the last thing I want to do is end up being your death. Willow's not your blood, she's mine."

Shade spoke. "She may not be my blood but," he paused, searching for his next words carefully, "let's just say she means a lot to me."

Waya smiled. "I know she does, and you mean a lot to her, too." Waya turned and began to pace around, scanning the woods for any sign of the men they were pursuing. "I know you've gotten to know Willow pretty well lately, but there's still a lot about her you don't understand. Her marriage really messed her up, as I've said, but then her brother dying right after it—she's been in a fragile state lately. She was taking a lot of prescription drugs, not abusing them really, just taking what the damn doctors told her to, but it still felt wrong to me. She finally weaned herself off of them, or at least I think she did, hell, I'm not sure, maybe I should have been paying more attention to her."

Shade put his hand on Waya's shoulder, "I think you did a pretty damn good job of looking out for her, and from what I've seen, a good job of raising her. And you have to deal with this ghostly swamp bullshit too? Hell, I think you're father of the year considering all you've been through."

Waya patted Shade's shoulder. "I thank you for saying

that, I do, but you don't know everything. I just should have paid attention to her. I feel like I neglected her to spend time with my son, because it was so much easier for me to relate to him, and now that he's gone I realize I may have done her a disservice. But the thing is, I'm really worried about her state of mind. We don't know what she's been through today, and she's been in a fragile state anyway, I'd hate to think those bastards could do something to finally break her. Hell, I wonder if she'd be better off broken or dead, and I feel like a total bastard for even thinking that way."

Shade shook his head, "It's natural to feel that way. Trust me, I've seen some guys that I think would have been better off dead, sometimes it's sad but true. But Willow won't be one of them. We'll get her back, I promise."

Waya smiled at Shade. "Don't make promises you can't keep, Kemosabe."

Shade smiled back when the gunshots filled the air, this time nearby. The two paused and listened as the shots rang out, at first shotgun blasts, and then automatic weapon fire. A loud explosion punctuated the gunfire. They could also hear yelling and screaming, but it was faint it was hard to determine exactly what they were hearing. Neither said a word, but both of them grabbed their bags and headed towards the sounds in a rush.

Richard awakened, the room eventually coming back into view. He didn't wake up the way one would normally would, but instead consciousness crept up on him, the room going from pitch black to bright, as if someone was turning the dimmer on a light switch. He saw he was still in the living room in the recliner. The only other person still in the room was Willow, who appeared to be sleeping on the couch. Everyone else was gone, including Bones. The bags and guns, however, were still just as they had been left.

The crazy rednecks drugged us, Richard thought as he cleared the cobwebs. He wondered what exactly was going on, because if they had meant to harm them, why did they just leave them here, and why would they leave the guns nearby? It didn't even appear they had been through the bags, and if robbery had been a motive the family would surely have been happy to find the cash stowed away there.

Richard thought perhaps his tolerance for drugs had been underestimated. He had pretty much tried every drug that existed, and most of them several times. His rape fetish had also made him somewhat of an expert on date rape drugs, and he had ingested them himself several times just so he'd have a better idea of what the experience would be like for his 'dates', so to speak. Therefore, it would take a much higher dose of narcotic to take him out than a normal person. He felt as though he had been drugged with something familiar, and was very thankful he had been.

There were noises and voices coming from the other end of the trailer, but he couldn't tell exactly who it was or what was being said. He very quietly checked his M16 out, and found it loaded and in good working order. He did the same with the shotgun on the coffee table, once again finding the gun undisturbed. He assumed Bones still had the Desert Eagle with him, wherever the hell he was.

Richard listened, and was able to determine both male and female voices, and sometimes laughter. There were also other noises coming from back there, some bangs and other sounds. *Are they just back there partying? Maybe the lemonade was just some kind of party drug and Bones handled it best, so the four of them are in the bedroom getting to know one another. That would explain why they didn't rob us or bother to take our guns.*

He decided to err on the side of caution and treat the situation as hostile, at least for right now. He got the two bags and set them on the floor near the front door, and he slung the M16 across his back by the strap, keeping the shotgun as his current weapon of choice. He looked down the hall and saw only one door at the end, most likely an add-on. *Those horny bastards probably converted the whole end of this place into a sex dungeon or some shit.* Richard grinned and shook his head as he stepped down the hall, stopping a second to be sure Willow was still out. Her steady breathing led him to believe she was still in a deep sleep, so he turned his attention to whatever waited at the end of the hall. His first guess was a sex dungeon, but his second was a meth lab. Maybe it was even a sex lab/meth dungeon or something equally bizarre. From what he'd seen in this swamp, hell, from what he'd seen in this *trailer*, nothing would surprise him.

The door was made of unfinished plywood with a golden doorknob. He cautiously put his ear to the door, the voices inside getting louder, and he could now identify Red, Malinda and Carol. He listened closer and sure enough, he heard Bones, but it sounded like Bones was moaning. *You old dog,* Richard thought as he reached for the door knob.

Just before his hand touched the knob, the door was abruptly flung open and Carol stood before him. She had her head turned away and was talking to someone behind her, but what really shocked Richard was the way she was dressed. She had on a large rubber apron, and black rubber gloves that came up to her elbows. She was wearing what appeared to be black combat boots, and her hair was pulled back in a ponytail. Clear goggles were on her forehead, held in place by black nylon straps. What disturbed Richard the most, however, was the fact she was covered in a thick red liquid that was surely blood.

"I can drag the little bitch back here by myself, don't you worry none. I'll be right back!" Carol said before turning and seeing Richard standing in the hallway with the shotgun. Her smile faded and her eyes widened as she jumped back, slamming the door before Richard even had a chance to react. "Oh shit, daddy, he's up and he's got a damn gun!" she exclaimed as the door slammed.

Richard raised the shotgun to blow his way into the room when holes began to explode in the door as he was fired upon from the other side of the door. Huge chunks of wood were blown away as the person fired randomly. He now knew where the .50 caliber had gone, because there was no doubt this was the familiar pistol spitting death at him from the end of the mobile home.

Richard hit the ground, stomach first, as this wasn't the first time he'd been fired upon. He counted the shots and soon seven were fired, the door Swiss cheese by this point. Taking the chance that no other guns were behind the door, Richard rushed in, kicking the doorway, which fell to pieces as he brought the shotgun up to fire. The sight that greeted him froze him in his tracks.

All three members of the family were present, and all dressed similar to Carol. Richard was still professional enough to ignore the other horrors in the room and focus instead on the immediate danger of Red, who had managed to pop out the empty clip and was just sliding a fresh one in as Richard shot him, the buckshot catching him in the midsection and ripping him apart as he fell to the ground.

Carol gave an inhuman scream and snatched up a bloodied sledgehammer from the ground, lifting it over her head and charging, ready to bring the heavy metal down and avenge her father. *How the hell can such a small girl handle that big ass hammer like that?* Richard thought as he fired again, catching Carol in the chest and slamming her backwards, ending her charge.

"You son-of-a-bitch, I'll kill you!" Malinda said, grabbing a butcher knife and slashing at Richard. She was much faster than he realized, and managed to slice his left arm before he adjusted and fired again, catching Malinda full in the face with the shotgun blast.

Richard checked all three family members, and didn't examine the room until he was certain they were all dead. Then he began to survey the chamber of horrors he had entered.

It was too much for the mind to process. This end of the mobile home had been converted to a combination slaughter house and bedroom. There was a double bed on one wall, and the area around the bed had been decorated as a married couple's bedroom. On the opposite wall, there was a frilly bed, and the area was decorated like a teenaged girl's bedroom, complete with posters of pop stars and stuffed animals. In the middle of the room however, was a worktable along with an assortment of tools that would normally be found in a butcher shop. Most items were on the wall, arranged on a pegboard.

Richard took the time to examine Bones, who was hanging from the ceiling by both arms. He was so tall that his feet were still on the ground, his legs bent to accommodate his large frame. The problem was, Bones was now living up to his namesake. From his waist down, Bones was nothing but a bloody skeleton. Blood and tiny bits of flesh covered his hip bones and leg bones as they hung beneath his torso, which appeared to be untouched. He wasn't wearing a shirt, and Richard assumed he had been stripped before they had started work on him. He walked over and found a drain directly under Bones' body, which allowed the blood to drain out of the room, although to where, Richard didn't want to speculate.

There was also a freezer in the room, and Richard mentally assured himself he would not open it, ever. He did inspect the work table, as something was on it. There were freezer bags covering the table, and the freezer bags contained fresh cuts of meat. It was Bones. They were butchering him and freezing him as one would a hog.

Richard fought the urge to vomit, his violent background being the only thing preventing it. He had seen and done some terrible things, but this made all of them pale in comparison. Richard heard a moan and almost jumped out of his skin. He aimed the shotgun at the bodies, going from all three to find out who was still alive. They were all quite dead. He heard the moan again, and this time looked at Bones. He squinted and walked to him. *No fucking way, that couldn't have been him, half his body is gone, no way.*

Another moan sounded, and this time Richard knew it was Bones. He saw a glassy-eyed expression on Bones' face, but he was still alive. Bones had a deep crater on the side of his bald head, and Richard reached the conclusion someone had bashed him in the head with the sledgehammer and tried to kill him just like a bull in a slaughterhouse. However, they had done a piss poor job and left him alive. And then decided to butcher him alive.

Bones moaned again, louder this time. Richard shook his head in disgust. He could only hope the blow to the head, combined with the drugs, was enough to keep Bones unaware of what happened to him, but he had a horrible feeling it had not. He began to shake with horror and rage, and pulled the shotgun up, firing right into Bones throat and ending his suffering.

Richard staggered from the room, rendered numb by what he had just seen and experienced. He walked down the hall. Willow was still on the couch, but she appeared to be stirring. He grabbed the two bags and sat one on the recliner and the other on the sofa. He was the sole survivor, so the money was all his now. He dumped all the money into one bag, and pulled out some shotgun shells and reloaded. He kept the M16 slung over his shoulder, and threw the now stuffed bag over his opposite shoulder. He walked over to Willow and shook her shoulders, trying to rouse her.

"Come on, we've got to get out of here," he said, slapping her cheeks firmly.

She blinked, coming out of her haze. He took her hand and helped her up, but as soon as she stood her legs collapsed beneath her, and she fell onto the coffee table. Richard pulled her up again, not noticing she had managed to palm a steak knife that had been left on the coffee table for lemon peeling if needed. She slipped it into her pocket as she put an arm around his back, pretending to be more out of it than she was. The medication she had been on had also raised her tolerance, and therefore she was also handling the drug a lot better than would have been expected. Richard heard a commotion outside as they neared the door, so he stepped to the side to peek out of the window, pulling the curtain aside just slightly with his hand, Willow clinging to his opposite shoulder.

What he saw outside chilled him to the bone. So the other trailers in the park had all been occupied after all, but instead of the normal appearing family of this trailer, the others all appeared to be disfigured monsters. Richard was sure the denizens now pouring out of the various mobile homes must have been the product of years of inbreeding, as he saw numerous deformities on every single person outside. They were also all carrying weapons of some sort—axes, pitchforks, knives, sickles, clubs, boards—basically anything that could be used to maim. He didn't see any guns yet, but he had to assume the worst. He couldn't count the number of people he saw heading towards the trailer, but he knew they had to outnumber the bullets he had left.

Willow was watching wide-eyed. She had been debating sliding the steak knife into Richard's throat and making her escape, but once again a new development forced her to rethink her plan. She had survived one of the most dangerous days anyone could have ever experienced, so the last thing she wanted to do was blow it now. She once again decided the best thing to do would be to stick with Richard until they got through this latest nightmare, and then wait for her next opportunity to get away.

Richard inspected the sea of mutated humans, and wondered how the hell Malinda and Carol had managed to come out of this. They were straight out of an adult magazine, and everyone else here was a deformed monster. Even Red was handsome compared to these melon heads. He assumed it was either a freak occurrence of nature, or more likely some outsiders had been captured and bred to come up with normal-looking humans. He guessed that the two women had seen them coming and basically acted as bait. He also wondered now if Willow's fate had been food—or something much worse.

"Can you stand?" Richard said, still watching as the crowd neared the trailer.

Willow nodded, and then when she saw Richard wasn't looking at her and was still scanning the mob outside, she answered in the affirmative.

"Then stay right with me, if you fall behind I don't think I can save you this time, and I think in this case I'm the lesser of two evils," Richard said. Willow might have debated that with him. "Get behind me and hold onto my belt. Don't let go and keep a tight grip, I know this is going to get hairy."

Willow let go of Richard and stood directly behind him and gripped his belt as ordered. This would be the perfect time to plunge the knife directly between his shoulder blades, but she knew keeping her cool was the key to her survival, so she kept the urge under control, at least for the moment.

Richard put the M16 on single-shot mode, and held it in one hand, the shotgun in the other. He still had the bag on his shoulder. He knew he could fight better with Willow holding the bag, but he'd been through hell today, and no way was he going to lose that money. He'd sooner lose the girl.

The throng had by now gathered around the trailer, but had yet to attempt entering the door. Richard did a quick survey around and it appeared the entire trailer was surrounded, so one exit would be as good as the other. He figured he might as well use the front door.

"Okay, its go time," Richard said, kicking the door open.

As soon as the door opened, a yell went up from the mob and they rushed the door. Thankfully, it just had the one set of narrow steps, so Richard began firing into the throng with the shotgun, the buckshot striking the nearest mutant in the face, a young one with a pumpkin-shaped head and long, stringy hair, brandishing a small sickle. The force of the blast slammed his body back, knocking down several of the group. Richard didn't hesitate and began to fire with both weapons as he used the bodies as stepping stones, stepping right onto them as he made his way among the mob.

Willow held on as best she could, losing her footing a few times but managing to keep a tight grip on Richard's belt and hauled herself right back up. Richard spun the weapons around, firing at random and clearing a path through the mass of humanity. Richard was spinning in a slow circle and firing at random, trying to keep any mutants from attacking him from behind, or attacking Willow. He knew at this point she was a severe liability, and if she went down he wasn't going to stop for her. She knew this as well, and her hands gripped his belt in a death grip.

A girl with one eye and no mouth charged with a pitchfork. Richard used the rifle to bat the pitchfork to the side and then caught her in the chest with a shotgun blast, her fall managing to knock down a few of the others.

It was slow going as the two fought through the crowd. One young boy with a machete managed to cut Richard's arm before Richard put a bullet right into his forehead. At least Richard thought he was a boy, he had the appearance of an eight-year-old, other than the long gray beard sprouting from his chin.

The group appeared to have no idea how to work as a unit. They were stabbing and injuring each other more than anything else. The ones in the back just wanted to get to the front where the newcomers were, and if it meant killing a few of their fellow trailer park residents, then so be it.

As Richard and Willow neared the chain-link fence, they had a problem. The sheer amount of human bodies were cutting them off. There were people between them and the fence on each side, as they had neared the corner of the fence without realizing it. The people were packing them in so tightly they had nowhere to go. Richard used the shotgun to kill a few more of them, buying him a few precious seconds. A mutant with no face rushed at him with a butcher knife, and Richard used the shotgun as a club to bash him to his knees before putting a bullet from the rifle right in the top of his head. When his body hit the ground Richard had a split second, where he thought he saw eyes and a mouth on the back of the mutant's skull peeking at him from beneath the hair.

Richard knew he had to think of something, and fast. Willow was kicking out at the mutants as best she could, but did not want to let go of Richard for even a second. One of the mutants chopped at her leg with an ax, just deep enough to bring about blood, as she cried out.

Richard was searching desperately for some way out, when he saw a glimmer of hope. On the back of the trailer nearest them, was a huge propane tank. Richard hoped the mass of human meat between him and the tank would shield him from the blast, but he had no other options. He aimed the M16 at the tank and fired shot after shot directly at it. After a few pings, he heard a spark and dove to the ground as the tank exploded, a huge fireball engulfing the area as the force of the explosion sent bodies flying everywhere.

The screams of the burning filled the air as Richard and Willow hit the ground, the bodies of the dead and dying covering them. Richard began to crawl along, heading towards the fence. He fired the shotgun several times, hearing it click on empty, but by this point they were at the fence. Richard used the M16 to kill a few more mutants, and then draped their bodies over the fence and climbed over them. Willow held on for dear life and also used the bodies, both of them landing on the other side.

Without so much as a glance back, Richard grabbed Willow's arm and pulled her along, running deep into the woods as they heard another explosion, and then another. The fire was spreading to the other tanks, and before long the entire trailer park would be engulfed in flames.

They traveled without any idea of direction other than putting distance between themselves and the trailer park from Hell and Richard thought about what had just happened. The trailer park itself felt surreal, a stereotype of the worst trailer park imaginable. The entire day was that way, as if they had been dropped into the middle of a horror movie. Richard wasn't sure what exactly to make of his profound realization, but he would be damn glad to get the hell out of this place.

They found themselves climbing a small hill, and when they reached the top, the vantage point gave them a great view of the trailer park. The entire park was indeed burning, and the screams of the dying mutants could be heard clearly. Both he and Willow watched curiously, as none of the mutants crossed over the fence. They were all just bunched up along the fence lines as the fire washed over them, cooking them alive. Why wouldn't they leave the fenced-in area? This explained why they hadn't been pursued. Could they be like chickens in a coop, having known this cage for so long they were either too scared to venture out of it, or didn't even know leaving was possible? Richard had no answer, and just watched as the trailer park burned.

FIFTEEN

THE EIGHTIES

The Fowler family walked along the path, each member of the family carrying something that would be used for their camping trip. The family of four was going to spend the night in the woods, roughing it. The so-called 'campers' who had their trailers with running water and VCR's weren't true campers. Even worse were the ones who 'roughed it' by staying in cabins much nicer than their own homes in many cases. A true camping trip involved no power, no toilets, and tents. A campfire and lanterns were all the light you needed, and a cooler the only modern convenience. Greg Fowler was going to teach his children—ten-year-old son Trey and eight-year-old daughter Daisy—what camping was about. His wife Doreen had her own thoughts about camping and they did, in fact, involve a real toilet, but she decided to humor her husband and allow him his one night each summer in the wilderness.

The family had started out at a state park, but Greg had wanted to be sure they got out away from civilization, so the family had started down a random trail and they had been following it forever. The land had gotten swampy, and Doreen had gotten a little worried. They were definitely lost, but they had walked a straight path the entire way, so she assumed just by following the same path out they should end up where they started. She had no idea they had wandered into Black Swamp.

Greg was carrying most of the load, the biggest tent on his back and the small cooler in his hand. Doreen had the kids' tent on her back, and the rest of the supplies such as sleeping bags, lanterns, food, and other essentials, had been distributed between the four of them. Greg had his ax and Trey had his survival knife, just in case they ran into any snakes or bears out here. Snakes were a possibility, bears not so much. The family didn't own any guns, but they wouldn't have been allowed in the park anyway

Greg stopped when they reached a clearing. There were large oak trees over the area and the ground wasn't too spongy, so it would be a great place to make camp. Greg was an accountant by trade, and his horn-rimmed glasses and balding head even made him look like one.

"Okay, kids, I think this is the place. Let's get the tents up and get a fire going, those s'mores aren't going to make themselves!" Greg said, smiling as he began to unpack his rucksack

The kids cheered and everyone began to do their part. In less than an hour both tents were up and the fire was blazing. It was still daylight, but Greg never got to build fires since they lived in an apartment complex downtown, so he was always obsessive about getting the campfire going.

The family did some exploring around the campsite, finding different insects and animal tracks—some familiar, some not. They also played Frisbee and then had a great game of hide-and-seek, the forest providing them with many hiding places. All in all, it was the perfect day out with the family.

That night they roasted hot dogs over the fire and then had the promised s'mores. The kids began to doze and when they were ordered to bed, even though they protested, they were so worn out from the day's activities the protests were half-hearted at best. As the kids went into their tent and turned out the lanterns, Greg and Doreen got out the bottle of wine they had smuggled in for the occasion and had a romantic evening by the fire.

"You know, we have done pretty well for ourselves haven't we? I mean, we couldn't ask for better kids, I got that promotion at the firm last year, we already have college funds set up, and things are fine," Greg said as he sat near the fire, his arm around Doreen.

"We've worked hard for what we've got. I say we've earned every bit of it," Doreen said, kissing him on his cheek.

"Well m'lady, methinks the offspring are asleep, what say we retire into the tent for some grown-up fun?" Greg said, doing a goofy old English accent.

"Why, sir, what kind of lady do you take me for?" Doreen said, playing along.

"Why, a trollop, of course!" Greg said, earning him a playful slap.

Doreen climbed into the tent as Greg checked the fire, deciding it would safely burn out for the night before joining Doreen in the tent. He zipped up the tent and climbed into the sleeping bag with her, kissing her deeply.

As soon as their lips met, they began to hear the kids giggling in their tent outside. They both stopped kissing and sighed. They waited to see if the kids would go back to sleep, and when they heard no further giggling, Greg kissed her again. Giggling rang out yet again.

"Kids, go to sleep!" Greg yelled, joking but serious at the same time. The kids went silent and Greg ran his hand down Doreen's back. Even louder giggling disturbed the night.

"Trey, Daisy, come on kids, it's late, we are getting up early tomorrow. Get some rest." Doreen called out, sternly this time. After a few minutes of waiting, the kids were silent again.

"Now, where were we?" Greg said, kissing Doreen's neck his time. The kids laughed louder than ever, the sound echoing through the night.

"If you're not quiet and get to sleep right now, I'm going to—" Doreen started, but was cut off by Greg.

"Hey, you little bastards! Shut the fuck up or I'm going to whip both your asses!!" Greg yelled, shocking Doreen into silence.

Greg never cursed or even raised his voice to the children, so this outburst came as a total surprise. The glow from the fire penetrated the thin walls of the tent, and for just a second Doreen could have sworn she saw Greg's eyes flash red. It had to be a trick of the firelight, but the effect was eerie. She lay in stunned surprise as Greg listened for any sound the kids made. He was breathing heavily, and she could swear he was grunting. Thankfully, the kids were silent, the outburst having scared them more than it surprised her.

Doreen finally spoke, "That was a little uncalled for, don't you think? I mean this is a vacation, I'd expect them to be a little rambunctious."

"Just shut up for a second, God, do you ever stop talking?" Greg whispered as he grabbed her by the hair, pulling her head back roughly and kissing her neck. Doreen gave a small shout of surprise, never having known Greg to be so aggressive. She was wondering whether she liked it or not when he began to bite her neck, softly at first but then harder to the point it hurt. Before she could protest, however, the kids giggled again.

"Goddamn it! That's it!!" Greg said, jumping up and heading out of the tent.

"Greg, what are you going to do?" Doreen asked, this sudden personality change worrying her.

"I'm going to discipline those brats of ours!" Greg said as he unzipped the tent. Doreen knew it had to once again be a trick of the firelight playing on his face, but she could see his eyes were glowing red, and also, why did his teeth all appear sharp, as though each one had been filed to a point? She decided she'd have to lay off the wine next time. She was obviously getting too old for it and her mind was playing tricks.

She heard the kid's tent being unzipped, and the kids groggily answering Greg as he yelled at them. She couldn't be sure from there, but it sounded like they were protesting that they had even been giggling, and they did sound like they had just woken up. But if it hadn't been them giggling, what had they heard?

Suddenly the kids began to scream, the most bloodcurdling sound Doreen had ever heard in her life. Greg's yells echoed out over the screams, but his voice was so hoarse and muffled she couldn't even understand a word he was saying. *Was that even Greg's voice? That deep and gravelly? It sounded nothing like him.*

The kids screamed a little longer before the screams were cut short. She also heard other sounds over the screams, sounds she couldn't recognize. Melons being smashed, or something similar. Just what the hell was Greg doing out there? She wanted to get up and check, but found herself unable to. She was rooted to the spot, her body just not responding to the signals she was sending it.

The tent was violently ripped open, and Greg stood there, the ax in his hand. The moon wasn't very bright, but it appeared as though something was dripping from the ax, and Greg's eyes seemed to be glowing an even brighter red. He stood there in silence a few seconds before speaking.

"I hated to do it, but I punished them. They should be quiet the rest of the night while we have our fun." Greg said, his voice sounding absolutely nothing like him, and barely sounding human at all. It had an otherworldly quality to it—an evil quality.

Doreen forced herself to turn the lantern on. When it illuminated Greg, she saw he was covered in blood, and the ax in his head was also covered in blood and pieces of *something*. She tried to scream but couldn't as she saw Greg's face. His eyes were indeed glowing red, and his entire facial structure had changed. This was no longer her husband—this was something demonic. He dropped the ax and pulled Trey's survival knife from his pocket.

"And we are going to have so much fun." Greg said as he entered the tent. As he stepped closer, Doreen managed to scream.

SIXTEEN

Richard and Willow stood at the top of the hill and Richard turned this back to the burning trailers as he spoke to her. He had decided they didn't have much daylight left, and they would be better off spending the night here rather than try to make their way through this damn swamp at night. This hilltop was the highest ground he had spotted since they had gotten stuck here in the first place.

"Okay, here's how it's going to work," Richard said, facing Willow who was sitting down, leaning against a tree. "Tonight we're going to just sleep up here on top of this hill. Hopefully it's safe enough so we shouldn't get into too much trouble, and I should be able to see if any damn mutants or zombies or such bullshit comes after us. And tonight, you are going to show your appreciation to me for keeping your ass alive all day. And I can tell from looking at you, you are good at showing appreciation." Richard rubbed the back of Willow's cheek with his hand in mock affection. She didn't bother pulling away, just gave him a look that shot daggers in his direction. The hardness of the knife was soothing in her pocket, and she knew the first chance she got she was going to bury it deep in Richard's throat.

Shade and Waya made their way to the trailer park easily. When the church had burned, they had been much further away, and the church was also a much smaller blaze. The trailer park had been packed with several highly combustible mobile homes, not to mention the many propane tanks, and it had managed to blaze long enough for the pair to reach it.

The two stood just outside of the range of the flames, watching as the bodies and buildings burned. The fire burned right to the fence and then stopped, like it had reached some type of invisible barrier and could go no further. They stared, trying to determine how many bodies were burning and who or what they could have been.

"You have any explanation for any of this? Who they are, why the damn fire won't spread past the fence, any of this?" Shade asked as he watched the pyre, mesmerized by the dancing flame.

Waya shook his head, "I have no clue. It probably has no explanation, just like all the other shit in this damned place. If a snake lady that turns people to stone can live out here, I guess we shouldn't be so surprised by a burning trailer park."

Shade searched around, trying to find out if the men they were trailing could be nearby. "So do you think Willow...I mean the fire...could she—?" Shade began, never quite able to voice the horrible thought.

Waya shook his head once again, "If she had died, I think I'd have known. She's still alive, and I think she's close."

Both men began to scout around the area, searching for any clues that could lead them to their quarry. Shade saw a hill nearby, and he thought he saw something down at the bottom of it, on the opposite side. He got his binoculars out, and even though he should have been used to it by now, he was still shocked by what he found. He had seen some big ones before, mostly in Central America, but never anything near this size. Even the ones around a foot long were eerie, but one this size was pure death.

As Shade panned around the area, he saw movement, this time at the top of the hill. When he panned his binoculars up, his heart began to pound and his breath became shallow. It was her, Willow, and standing with his back to them were one of the captors. He tried his best to see if any others were nearby, but he only saw the two of them. He didn't want to even let Waya know yet, until he had a solid plan in mind. This was not the time to rush in unprepared, and he knew Waya would become very emotional when he found out his daughter was so close.

"Waya, can I hold your hunting rifle please?" Shade asked. Waya looked at him quizzically but asked no questions, handing him the bolt action rifle as Shade handed him the binoculars in return. "Now, don't do anything stupid. I want your word you'll stay put until I say we go."

Waya was puzzled but hopeful now. "Sure, sure, what is it? Tell me?"

"Look up at the top of the hill, and keep quiet, don't move or say a word." Shade said as he used the scope on the rifle to zoom in on the man on the hill.

Waya saw the man at first, and then saw Willow sitting on the ground. He at first just studied Willow, trying to determine her condition. She appeared fine from here, but he wouldn't be satisfied until he saw her up close. He then panned around the same as Shade had, searching all over and around the hill for more of the thugs. Somehow he managed to miss what Shade had spotted earlier at the bottom of the hill, but no additional men were nearby.

Shade was still watching the man through the scope, not sure of the exact distance. It wouldn't be an easy shot, but it was by no means impossible. He wanted a head shot, but at this distance it was too risky. A body shot would have to do, but he had no doubt with the high caliber rifle that would be enough.

"Waya, I'm going to let you make this call. I can make this shot. If this is the only one of those bastards left, then I pop him, we go get Willow and go home. But, if one of his buddies is around, and he gets to Willow before us, I can't guarantee what will happen. I can wait here and let you try to move in, but I don't know how long he'll be there. Plus, it's getting dark soon, and if we don't do it now, we may not have time to do it. It's your call, buddy. What do we do?" Shade asked, having been sighting in on Richard with the scope throughout the entire conversation.

Waya paused to think.

Richard was giving a speech to Willow by this time, going on and on about how lucky she was to be alive, and how he was the only reason. He was also on a rant about losing his friends today, and a general rant about his terrible luck and how much he hated the swamp. Willow was just letting him talk and planning when to stick him with the knife when something down near the burning mobile homes caught her attention.

She thought she saw Shade and her father. She glanced back up at Richard, hoping he hadn't followed her eyes. He wasn't even watching her, instead lost in his ranting and waving his arms in the air at this point. Willow stole another glance down, and saw Shade aim a rifle at Richard. She became excited now and felt true hope for the first time since she had been captured. Richard began to pace now, and he could turn around and spot Shade and Waya at any second. She had to do something.

"You're right. If it wasn't for you, I'd be dead. You fought Hell itself for me, and I want to reward you, any way you like," she stammered, regretting her choice of words. It sounded canned, and there was no way Richard would fall for it.

Richard stopped pacing and stared down at Willow, smiling now. "I guess you're coming around after all. You know, there's a lot to be said for the unwilling, but every now and then it would be nice to just tell a bitch to do something and have her do it. I think this night in the swamp may turn out not so bad after all."

A gunshot echoed in the swamp, and the bullet smacked Richard in the back, right on his shoulder blade, slamming him forward but not off of his feet as he stumbled. Willow's entire body jerked involuntarily. Even though she was halfway expecting the shot, it still came as a surprise.

Richard stumbled around dumbfounded, wondering how she had managed to shoot him in the back when he was right there staring at her the entire time. He then turned around to face the direction of Shade and Waya, but before he could look down, another shot rang out, this time striking Richard full in the chest and knocking him flat on his back, where he lay completely still.

Willow blinked, still unsure as to what happened. The M16 was lying nearby, so she grabbed it up. She had seen too many things in this swamp. She didn't want to survive this day of torment only to be eaten alive by a damn giant snake or something similar. She barely glanced at Richard's body as she stood up, throwing the gun down. The last thing she needed was for Shade to see her with the gun and think she was one of the criminals and shoot her. That would be one shitty end to her day.

She walked over to the edge and waved, trying to get a good look at Shade and her father. She was grinning so hard her mouth hurt as she waved her arms, tears of joy streaming down her cheeks. She couldn't exactly make out what they were doing, but from their hand signals it appeared the two men were telling her to stay there and they would come get her. She didn't relish the idea, but liked the idea of wandering around in the swamp alone even less, so she gave them a thumb's up and prepared to wait. They weren't very far away, so hopefully the wait would be a short one.

Waya had told Shade to take the shot, and he had done so, striking Richard right in the back, and when he didn't go down, he gave him a shot in the chest for good measure. Shade kept the rifle ready in case any more thugs popped up, but none did. Either they had split up before now, or the rest had been killed by the many hazards of the swamp. Shade hoped it was the latter, and good riddance to the sons-of-bitches.
    The two of them watched Willow waving and they waved back, using hand signals to let her know to wait, and they would be coming for her. She gave them a thumb's up in response, and the two grinned and started her way.
    "See, old man? Nothing to it," Shade said, smiling with mock bravado. "Now let's go get her."

The two managed to make their way over to the hill with no trouble, although Shade did warn Waya about what he had seen at the bottom of the hill and told him to be alert. They were on guard the entire time, but reached the hill without encountering anything, be it a monster or any of the bank robbers. They climbed the hill to find Willow waiting for them.

Willow had sat back down to rest, still watching carefully for any creatures, the gun near her side. When she saw Shade and Waya coming up the path that led to the top of the hill, she jumped up to greet them. Unfortunately, so did Richard, who pulled out the survival knife he had managed to keep and grabbed Willow from behind.
    Willow let out the most bloodcurdling scream she could manage, as at no point during the horror-filled day had she been as scared or surprised as when Richard grabbed her from behind

and pressed the cold steel of the sharp knife against her throat. Shade and Waya saw what was happening and both went for their guns, but Richard yelled out to stop them.

"Drop those fucking guns or this little squaw loses her goddamn head right now!" he yelled, a tight grip on her, the knife so tight against her throat, blood was already welling around the edge of the blade.

Even men with Shade and Waya's experience couldn't move fast enough to stop Richard before he could slash Willow's throat, and out here in the middle of nowhere there would be no way to save her once her veins and arteries opened up. They dropped their bags and their guns, raising their hands.

"Yeah, that's smart. I know what you're thinking, I kill this bitch, and you both kill me, so I die anyway right? After the fucking day I've had, I don't give a shit! Maybe I'd be happy to kill the little whore and check out smiling! Don't fuck with me. I am not in the mood!" Richard said, still keeping a tight death grip on Willow.

Shade noticed Richard was doing an expert job of shielding his own body with Willow's, even though he was much larger than her. This obviously wasn't the first time Richard had been in a standoff situation with a hostage, and the knowledge sickened Shade even further. The bastard had been wearing a bullet proof vest. He appeared to be coughing up blood, and even from this distance Shade could hear him wheezing, so he had broken some ribs and maybe punctured his lungs, but he hadn't killed him, and they were paying for that mistake now.

"Now listen, we've had a pretty shitty day too, and we just want the girl back," Waya said, telling the truth. "I don't give a shit about any bank money that's all insured anyway. I see that bag over there. I'm guessing that's the cash, right? You let the girl go, get your bag, and go your way, and we'll go ours. We aren't even cops, we're game wardens, and we just want the girl. Let the real police worry about catching you. As far as we're concerned, you walk. Deal?"

Willow eyed her dad incredulously. *After all the shit this bastard's done, he walks? The hell he will.* Willow had taken her fair share of self-defense courses, so she was just biding her time, and soon enough, her time was there. She slipped the knife from her pocket, Richard so fixated on Shade and Waya he didn't even notice. Shade saw what she was doing but didn't even give a hint of it away with his eyes. When Richard loosened his grip for just an instant, contemplating Waya's offer, Willow grabbed his forearm, hoping she'd be at least strong enough to hold his hand steady as she drove the steak knife up between her legs and into his crotch, burying six inches of serrated metal right between Richard's testicles.

The shock and pain was so great, he didn't even attempt to slash Willow, and instead loosened his grip just enough to wiggle free and dive for the ground. As Shade saw Willow stab Richard with the knife, Shade dove for the ground, snatching up his M16 and flipping to full auto in the same motion. He landed flat on his stomach and as soon as Willow was out of the line of fire he opened up with the machine gun, sending a horde of bullets at Richard before he had a chance to react.

Most of the slugs still caught Richard in the body armor —the impact breaking bone and giving him further internal injuries. Some of the slugs caught him in the arms, causing him to drop the knife. A few caught him in the legs and thighs, tearing away flesh upon impact. One even caught him in the cheek, tearing away the skin and exposing his teeth, and another grazed his skull.

Richard still didn't go down under the barrage, but the force of the impact did cause him to stumble backwards and finally fall off of the hill. Just as he fell, Shade's gun clicked on empty, and they heard Richards muffled groans as he went over the side. Shade took a second to slam a fresh clip into his rifle as they heard something rustling at the bottom of the hill from where Richard had fallen, and Richard's weak cries filtered up to them.

Willow ran over to Shade, giving him a bone-crushing hug and she cried against his chest. He hugged her back with one arm, holding the M16 in the other, as he kissed the top of her head. She was saying something, but it was unintelligible due to her sobs.

"It's okay, you're okay, it's all over now, you're fine," Shade repeated as Waya made his way over, smiling to see his daughter embracing Shade. She saw her father from the corner of her eye and ran over to embrace him, the two of them crying in a tearful reunion.

Shade took this opportunity to walk over to the edge of the cliff, peering over to see Richard in the mandibles of the giant centipede he had spotted earlier. In his years in the military, Shade had heard tales of the Death Crawlers—supposed centipedes up to ten feet long that could easily kill a man. This one was easily ten feet, and it had Richard tight in its fangs as it rolled around, wrapping its long body around its prey. Shade could see Richard's face in the twilight, his dead eyes wide open as foam poured from his mouth, the large amount of venom causing severe anaphylactic shock.

Shade contemplated just leaving the centipede to enjoy his meal, but he didn't want that thing loose in the swamp. He pumped the grenade launcher mounted on the bottom of his rifle and fired a grenade down onto the monstrous insect, blowing it in half. The two halves were also burning, as was the body of Richard. Shade watched the two insect halves thrash about as they burned before he was convinced both the insect monster and the human monster were truly dead.

He walked back over to Waya and Willow, who both smiled.

"Is he?" Willow asked, and Shade just nodded.

"Did you kill that—?" Waya asked, and Shade just nodded again.

Shade took a second to admire the swamp. It was getting dark, and night would be upon them soon. "What do you think? Should we head out or try to spend the night here?"

Both Willow and Shade waited to hear his verdict, as in this matter he was the decision maker. "We better stay here tonight. I can make sure we aren't bothered."

The two nodded and Shade got Willow some water as Waya made his preparations for the night. He took out a bag filled with some type of dust—salt, silver dust, and other herbs which only Waya knew. He sprinkled it around the hilltop in a circle, as well as over all of the trees on and near the hill. He explained this should keep out anything that tried to get in, but they would keep their guns handy just in case.

The three of them had a meager dinner of water and some stale beef jerky Shade and Waya had found in their bags, not even remembering they had put it there. Judging from its toughness, it had been left there from a prior trip. Regardless, they ate it ravenously, happy to have it. Shade and Waya questioned Willow, and were happy to hear that she had only suffered minor harm. They both listened intently as Willow explained all of the various trials and tribulations she had experienced, and both Shade and Waya knew when this was all over, they would need to have a long talk with Willow about the swamp.

They prepared to go to sleep, Willow between the two men. As they lay down, Willow grabbed both sides of Shade's head and gave him a good night kiss, a *real* one, as her tongue entered his mouth, shocking him. She giggled and curled up next to him. Even in the haunted swamp, the three were all worn out from the incredibly difficult day they had, and soon all three of them were asleep.

SEVENTEEN

Shade awoke just as the sun was rising, finding Waya already awake and gathering their items for the trip home. Willow was still asleep, and considering the day she'd had before, Shade could understand her exhaustion. Shade stood up and stretched, feeling quite refreshed. He'd slept in much less comfortable places on many of his SEAL missions, so this wasn't so bad.

Willow woke up when Shade stood, rubbing her eyes and yawning. It took a few seconds for her to put together where she was and what was going on, but she sat up and leaned back against the tree, still very groggy as she tried to come out of it.

Shade picked up his M16 and did a quick recon of the immediate area, including searching for the remains of Richard and the centipede. There was no sign there had been a fire in that area, and no remains of the centipede were visible. The bloated and burnt body of Richard was still there, although it appeared to have been mutilated. Something had been at his body during the night, but Shade had no sympathy for the killer's body.

Shade walked back over to examine the remnants of the burnt trailer park. It was all still there, the fire barely smoldering. It was basically just a huge pillar of ash, and there was nothing to indicate it had once been a trailer park or there were bodies burnt in the fire. Shade found that odd, but reminded himself that in Black Swamp, odd wasn't always so odd.

He stepped back across the line of powder Waya had put down the night before when something caught his eye. He walked along the trail, his stomach sinking a little at what he was seeing. All along the edge of the powder, there were tracks. Many different types of tracks. Some were large hoof prints, others human, others looked like deep claw marks. All through the night, they had been surrounded. By what, Shade didn't know and honestly didn't want to know, but it appeared as though many of the hellish denizens of the swamp had stopped by to check them out. Thank God for Waya's magic powder, otherwise the trio wouldn't have survived the night.

Shade walked back over to Willow, deciding it was best to try to conceal the tracks from her. Her state of mind was already fragile, and she didn't need anything else to worry about. Shade happened to glance up at the tree he had been sleeping under, and there were deep scratches along parts of it, apparently large claw marks. They had been stalked last night, and all three of them had slept right through it. At least, he assumed so. He saw Waya wolfing down the last of the jerky and drinking some water to chase it, and thought about walking over to see how his night had been. He took one step and changed his mind. If Waya wanted to discuss how he had passed the night, Shade would listen, but otherwise, he was just gonna keep his mouth shut. Some things he was better off not knowing.

He gave Willow some water and jerky and had some for himself. None of them had spoken yet, as they were appreciating the silence and trying to use the quiet to sort things out in their minds. The sun was up by now, and even though their watches were useless, Shade guessed it was around six a.m.

Waya was the first to speak. "We need to get going. I'm not exactly sure how far it is to the boat, and we all know how things go in this damned place."

Willow and Shade still didn't speak, just nodded as they followed Waya down the hill. Willow was still carrying the M16 Richard had dropped, even though Shade had offered her the use of his smaller sidearm. She had declined. After the things she had seen, she wanted heavier firepower for this leg of the journey,

Surprisingly, the trip to the boat presented no problems. Other than the damn humidity and the biting insects, they encountered nothing out of the ordinary. It was as if the swamp had thrown everything it had at them yesterday, and was taking this time to rest. Resting for a rematch would have been the way Shade would have put it.

Waya once again amazed Shade as he made his way directly for the boat, not even taking a wrong turn once. Willow also knew right where they were going, although whether it was some special talent or she was just doing a great job of following her father, Shade wasn't quite able to determine.

Waya was moving faster than Willow and Shade, in a hurry to get home to his wife who had to be worried sick by this point. Shade stuck behind Willow and Waya never got out of sight, so they were still traveling safely.

After several hours of traveling, the boat finally came into view. Waya grinned and rushed ahead, as Shade and Willow slowed down, adopting a leisurely pace since their goal was in sight and they were both tired. Shade was also slightly miffed, as he was still in peak physical condition and yet this girl was hanging right with him, and the old man was *surpassing* him. He might need to get back into shape once he found time.

They neared the bank and found Waya had already climbed into the boat and was checking things over. Once again, Waya's magic had saved them, as the boat was right where they had left it and undamaged. Shade and Willow stood on the bank and surveyed the area, hoping to spot anything dangerous before they got into the boat and began the voyage back to the station.

"You're still going to die out here." Meg said, appearing beside Willow.

Willow's mouth dropped as she ogled the girl. With all that had happened in the past twenty-four hours, she had totally forgotten about her. Meg just stared at her with no expression, her eyes dead. She was still wearing the same dirty dress.

"Who's your friend, Willow? Where did you come from, darlin'?" Shade said as he walked over and spotted Meg, still apprehensive about what happened on the playground but not wanting to scare the little girl.

Willow gaped at Shade, astonished, and even Meg's poker face broke as they both showed surprise at Shade's question.

"You can see her?" Willow asked, looking from Shade to Meg, and then back and forth. She was so surprised she didn't know what else to say.

Shade gave Willow a quizzical look. "Um, yes I can see her, she's standing right there. Is everything okay? Who is this girl?" Shade asked. He remembered the playground, and got a little apprehensive, but this waif surely didn't appear to be dangerous. She was frail and out in the middle of the day, how much trouble could she be?

Meg smiled at Willow, and then turned to smile at Shade.

"My name is Meg. Will you be my boyfriend?"

Shade smiled down at Meg as she smiled up at him, but then Meg was no longer a little girl. In less than a second, her skin turned an olive-green and shriveled up to the texture of parchment. Her hair fell out in one large piece to reveal pointed ears as her eyes turned solid black with no hint of anything but a dark pupil. Her hands also turned to claws—long, thin and sharp. But the worst part by far was her mouth. She sprouted fangs much too big for her mouth, and her entire jaw distended to support them, her mouth growing to the size of her entire face.

She hissed and sprang at Shade, who just managed to get the M16 up as she pounced. He had one hand around the barrel of the gun and the other on the stock as he fell onto his back. Despite her small size, the pint-sized predator was showing tremendous strength. The teeth were only inches from his face as he pushed her away with the gun, her long forked tongue coming out and licking his cheeks, getting a small taste before dug into the main course.

Willow cocked her gun and aimed it at the monster, but then Shade began to thrash around as he tried to keep her teeth from this throat, and Willow found herself afraid to take the shot for fear of hitting Shade. The two of them thrashed around a few seconds as Willow tried to find a shot, but nothing presented itself. She smashed at the back of the creature's skull a few times with the butt of the gun, but it had no effect at all. She knew soon she'd have to just take the shot, and pray she didn't hit Shade by mistake.

Just as Shade felt his arms getting tired and the monster reached his throat, Waya opened an entire container of salt and shoved it into the creature's mouth. The creature screamed as the salt acted as acid, melting the creature into sludge on contact. Almost too fast to see, the monster was gone, and Shade found himself instead covered in gooey ectoplasm.

He watched as the green slime dripped from his body. "Yuck, this is disgusting. Thanks, Waya." Shade said as he shook his hands, slinging the sticky material away from him. Before he could even stand up, even the ectoplasm was gone. Shade's clothing showed no sign it had ever been touched, but his skin still felt cold and clammy. There was absolutely no sign of the creature. All remnants were gone.

"What the hell was that thing?" Shade asked as he got back to his feet.

"Some type of specter or evil spirit. It's unusual to see them during the day, but as you can see, it's not impossible," Waya said.

"That little bitch had been following me around yesterday! She kept telling me I was going to die in this swamp. I got so caught up with the wasps and cannibals I forgot to mention her. Damn, that was stupid of me. She kept appearing, but I was the only one who could see her! Until you saw her, I half wondered if she was a figment of my imagination. Maybe that's another reason I forgot to mention her." Willow said, obviously upset with herself and taking the blame for what had just happened.

"Hey, you can't blame yourself for what happens out here. This place is shitty and things happen, whether you had told us or not, it wouldn't have changed anything. Now let's get the hell out of here. Your mom's worried sick," Shade said, his tone of voice putting an end to the discussion.

They all climbed into the boat, which started easily, and Waya began to pilot them back to the station. They had managed to recover the money, and they still had the weapons they had taken into the swamp. By all accounts, they had to consider things a success.

The boat made it into the lagoon without any further interference. Just as the boat was about to dock, there was a sudden splash, and something surfaced near right beside them. Waya and Shade jumped but it was just a large log. Then the automatic fire of an M16 split the air as Willow shot the log to pieces, sending splinters everywhere as she opened fire on what she had thought was a monster. Waya and Shade both ducked into the bottom of the boat when the shooting started, looking up at Willow surprised. She stopped firing when she realized she was killing a log, and gave them a sheepish look before shrugging as if to say *sorry!*

They made it onto the dock and Willow felt like kissing the ground. They all went inside as Willow made a beeline towards the bathroom in the apartment, specifically the shower.

"Shade, can you get me something of yours to wear? My clothes smell rank!" Willow said as she made her way into the bathroom.

"Sure," Shade said, walking into the bedroom after her. He froze when he saw she was already stripping, leaving her clothes in a trail behind her as she headed for the bathroom. She was in her underwear when she stepped inside, and Shade caught of a glimpse of her in a mirror over the dresser as she finished undressing. He couldn't help but stare at her perfect nude body as she turned the water on and checked its temperature.

"Hey, what the hell, man, I'm standing right here!" Waya said, coming up behind Shade and seeing what was going on. Shade jumped higher than he had during the entire battle with the monsters in the swamp as he was busted. His face flushed beet red as he hurriedly gathered a pair of his boxers and a t-shirt, dropping them on the bed for Willow before hurrying back outside, shutting the apartment door behind him.

"Um, I was just getting her something to put on, since she wanted to change her ass when she got out, I mean her clothes. She wanted to change her clothes!" Shade said, tongued-tied and blushing furiously.

Waya just shook his head. "You horny white devil, hands off my daughter!" he said as he laughed, glad to pay Shade back for some of the ribbing he had taken over the last few weeks.

Shade and Waya put the bag containing the money on the desk and sifted through it as Willow bathed. "Now, how the hell are you going to explain all this? We got the girl and the money back, but the bad guys are gone for good. I don't think they are going to buy the true story here," Shade said.

"Let me handle it, this isn't the first time something like this has happened, I got this," Waya said, patting Shade on the head like a child.

EIGHTEEN

Shade had assumed they would face a nightmare in trying to explain just what had happened to the bank robbers and how the money had been recovered, but true to his word, Waya handled all of it. He made one phone call, and everything was handled. The story on the news reported the SUV carrying the bank robbers had managed to crash into a lake, not in Black Swamp of course, but in Waya's normal jurisdiction, and Willow had managed to escape, and had managed to bring the money with her.

Willow ended up a minor celebrity as the brave girl who thwarted the murdering bank robbers and managed to recover all of the bank's money. But as most things go, the news soon moved on to other stories, and it was all mostly forgotten. The news had even shown them recovering the SUV, but no bodies were ever found. Shade wondered what would come of that, but Waya assured him that when it came to men like the four who had robbed the bank, nobody would care for long. And that turned out to be true, as not even the relatives of the men were very concerned about recovering their bodies. It had turned out too good be true, and Shade wondered who had been on the other end of Waya's phone call.

As the months passed, Shade found himself getting in tune with his job and also becoming closer to Willow. Her mother had been overjoyed to see her returned, and had made Waya and Shade both promise to never, ever, let her near that infernal Black Swamp again. They both found that an easy promise and they didn't plan on letting Willow near the place again anyway.

The entire horrible experience had been cathartic for Willow, as though seeing just how dark the world can be made her conclude that her life wasn't really all that bad. Waya had explained the Black Swamp to Willow as best he knew how, trying to gloss it over and not make it sound so bad. But Willow had seen too much, she knew that place was haunted, and that things happened there that could never be explained. If she ever saw the inside of Black Swamp again, it would be too soon.

Willow eventually began to open up to Shade, and the two were eventually in an official relationship, although both were still taking it slow. They were still two damaged people, and they hoped in healing themselves they could also heal each other. They also had time, and there was no need to rush. For all of Waya's ribbing, he really would have been proud to call Shade son-in-law, so he did what he could to make things easier for the two without being pushy. His wife, however, had to be called down repeatedly as she attempted to play matchmaker. Everyone took it good-naturedly, however, and no harm was done.

Shade still hated the Black Swamp with a passion, but he knew someone had to watch over it. He was there to do his best to keep the swamp under control, and see that it caused as little damage to the world as possible. He knew it was a losing battle, but at least it was his battle to lose.

NINETEEN

PRESENT DAY

"All right, troops, keep it down, I'm trying to read this map!" Scoutmaster Ernest Jones said as he studied the laminated map he held in his hands. He was in a boat with his entire troop, all twelve boys from his local Cub Scout chapter. Ernest was a middle-aged African American man with too much pudge around his waist and not enough hair on his head, but he loved mentoring kids and he loved the outdoors, which made him a great scoutmaster. He and the kids were all dressed in traditional scout garb with the shorts and hats. His troop was mainly made up of underprivileged kids of all races. Black, Hispanic, white, and even a few Asian boys were among the kids currently bouncing the boat around and making sure Ernest had as hard a time as possible to check the map.

The boys all ranged in ages from seven to nine, and the group was taking a boat ride to earn some of the various merit badges. They had set off from a nearby public boat ramp, but for some reason once Ernest had taken a turn down a narrow creek, his GPS had stopped working, his cell phone lost its signal, and even his damn wristwatch stopped, and it wasn't even digital. He wasn't sure if they had ended up in the damn Bermuda Triangle or what, but he wanted to at least get some quiet time to check the map over.

"Boys, come on, remember the scout's number one motto, shut the fuck up when the scoutmaster says to!" Ernest said, losing his temper for a split second. The scouts shut up immediately, shocked to hear the F-word. Then they all began to giggle uncontrollably at the word.

Ernest tossed the map down into the bottom of the boat,

unable to make any sense of it. He noticed they had somehow ended up right in the middle of some swamp. There were cypress trees draped with moss all around, and the waterway itself was quite narrow, only a few feet on each side of the boat separated it from the nearby bank. Ernest tried to decide whether he should back the boat up, or keep going forward. It would be hard to turn the boat around in this narrow channel, so he needed to decide soon.

The choice was then taken out of his hands as the water erupted near the boat, and a large creature grabbed onto the side of the boat and pulled itself up. The kids began to scream as Ernest just stared at the monster in silence, his brain not quite understanding just what he was seeing.

It was a merman—a humanoid fish monster. It had a basic human shape, but huge webbed claws for hands and its face was bug-eyed with a huge mouth full of sharp teeth, most resembling a piranha. It also had a large fin on its back, and a large tail which was currently splashing the water. The bottom half of the creature was still underwater, so Ernest wasn't sure if it had legs or fins, and at this point he didn't give a damn.

The boat had a small electric trolling motor, so it wasn't built for speed and a quick escape wasn't an option. Instead, Ernest snatched up a paddle and began to whack the creature in the face repeatedly. The paddle, however, was made of light wood and the impact wasn't doing much to dissuade the creature from climbing into the boat and making a meal of everyone inside.

As Ernest smacked the monster, others also began to crawl up the sides of the boat. Ernest found himself surrounded by the horrors from the depths, and wasn't sure what to do other than pray.

"Get on the bottom of the boat, kids! Huddle up, try to stay away from the sides!" Ernest said as he joined them in the center of the boat. He wasn't sure how much this would help since the monsters were soon going to be in the boat anyway, but it was all he could think to do.

One of the creatures raised its clawed hand, about to slash at the huddling scouts when the staccato sound of gunfire filled the air and the top of the creature's head exploded, sending it back down into the murky depths. The kids were already lying flat on the bottom of the boat, so Ernest laid on top of them, shielding their small bodies with his as best as he could as gunfire erupted, and more creatures were killed.

"Keep your heads down!" Ernest said as he watched the nearby bank to trace the sound of the gunshots. There was a man on the bank wearing what appeared to be a game warden's uniform and he was carrying a machine gun. He was firing at the mermen in short controlled bursts, expertly picking them off with head shots.

"Just stay low! If you can get the boat over to the bank that would help too!' Shade yelled as he continued to fire at the creatures, his M4 set on three round bursts as he concentrated on killing one at time. Head shots worked best, but his angle of fire made head shots difficult on some of the creatures, so he had to use body shots from time to time. It took more rounds to kill the monsters when he had to shoot the torsos, but they were still dying.

Ernest drove the boat over to the shore, just running it into the bank as the creatures now started to emerge onto land, going for Shade, who they knew was the immediate threat. The mermen did indeed have legs, although they were finned and had large clawed feet, similar to an alligator's and barely resembled human limbs at all.

Shade pulled his 9mm sidearm from its holster, holding it up to catch Ernest's eye, "Can you use this?" he asked as Ernest raised his hands to catch it.

Ernest nodded as Shade tossed him the pistol. Ernest cocked it and began to fire at the monsters, his time in the National Guard coming in handy as he helped Shade take care of the fiends. He wasn't sure how many rounds he had, so he tried to only fire a few shots and also aimed for the creatures' faces.

Shade's M4 clicked on empty just as a creature lunged for him, so he smacked the monster upside the head with the butt of the gun, knocking it backwards. Ernest saw what was happening and fired several shots into its back as Shade nodded his thanks and took the opportunity to reload, dropping the empty clip and slamming a fresh clip home. He gave the monster a burst to the head, killing it.

Ernest was also empty by this time. Without missing a beat, Shade tossed him a new clip, which Ernest used to kill some of the mermen. By now the numbers were dwindling, and after a few more shots the swarm ended. What was strange was every monster had ended up back in the water once killed—even the ones killed on the bank had slid back into the black pool. And they just disappeared, sinking below the surface never to be seen again. Other than some scratches on the boat and some claw marks on the ground, there was nothing to show the monsters had ever existed.

The scouts by now had stood up, most of them crying and wondering just what had just happened. They were all in a state of shock, as they hadn't broken down into chaos as most kids would have in this situation. Ernest and the scouts slowly climbed out of the boat onto the bank, Shade keeping an eye on the water as they did so.

"I'm going to need to drive your boat back to my dock, and then we'll find a way to drive you guys home," Shade explained. "We'll figure out a way to trailer your boat and return it to you later, but the important thing is getting you home."

Ernest nodded, but before he could speak, the water erupted in a huge waterspout, and a large, tentacled monstrosity emerged from the deep. It would be unfair to call the monster a squid, because its anatomy didn't fit the term. It had several tentacles coming from everywhere, not just one part of its body. It also had a huge mouth filled with large teeth, and its eyes were located right over its teeth, much the same way a human face is arranged. The monster was impossible for the mind to process accurately.

The creature roared and charged at them, its mouth large enough to swallow the entire troop in one gulp. Ernest didn't even bother firing at the creature with his pistol—he knew it would be futile. The tiny bullets couldn't harm this thing, and they didn't even have time to run before it would be upon them. They all stood frozen to the spot, like they knew the monster was going to eat them and they were accepting their fate.

Shade, however, did act. He pulled the pin on a grenade and tossed it right into the monsters gaping maw. The monster shut its jaws but too late, the grenade going deep into its gullet. A muffled explosion sounded, ripping a huge hole in the creature and sending a green, slimy residue over the entire scout pack, Ernest included. Shade was still standing a few feet away from the group, so he was lucky enough to avoid the gut shower.

The monster gave a weak bellow and slowly sunk beneath the surface, disappearing entirely, just as the smaller mermen had done. Whether the large monster was connected to the mermen in any way, or whether it was just coincidence they both appeared together, Shade had no clue, and really didn't care. He just hoped all of the damn things were dead.

Ernest and the troops just watched the beast sink into the water, staring silently while covered in the emerald goop. Once the monster was entirely out of sight beneath the black water, the troops all erupted in cheers, hands in the air and jumping all around, happy to be alive. Even Ernest joined in, wiping slime from his eyes as he jumped.

As was common in the swamp, within the seconds the green residue was gone, leaving nothing behind, not even a stain. Everyone was confused but happy to be clean, although a few members of the troop had been happy to be covered in monster guts.

Shade knew this would require some careful explaining. He decided he could talk to Ernest and convince him to play along and tell the kids the whole thing had been staged for their amusement, and the monsters had just been men in rubber suits. He wasn't sure if the kids would buy it, but in all honestly it was more believable than the truth. Ernest himself might require finesse, but Shade was sure the idea of top secret government experiments with biological warfare would work. He'd just have to be sure he scared Ernest into silence. If that failed, however, Waya had already said he could make a phone call in a situation like this, and anything that was said would never make it to credible news agencies. It would instead wind up on the pages of the tabloids, alongside the alien abductions and the kid raised by bats. As a matter of fact, things from the Black Swamp *had* made the tabloids several times over the years.

The kids were yammering amongst themselves as Ernest walked over to shake Shade's hand. "Thanks for the save. That was bad ass! I'm Ernest Jones, scoutmaster for this fine group here."

Shade shook his hand. "Nice to meet you, Ernest." Shade took a second to survey the water and the woods behind them, wanting to be sure nothing took them by surprise. Shade shook his head, "Oh, I'm sorry, how rude of me, I never introduced myself. I'm Shade Channing, and I'm the Game Warden of Black Swamp."

THE END...FOR NOW

The Game Warden of Black Swamp

The Game Warden of Black Swamp

Made in the USA
Monee, IL
23 December 2024